mu...
sone go...
and all...
cause

love
from
Susan
march '08

LAUGHING ALL
OVER THE WORLD

Compiled by
Jenny de Montfort

Published by Accent Press 2007

Copyright © 2007 Jenny de Montfort
Cartoons copyright remains with the artist

ISBN 9781905170059

Printed and bound in UK
by CPD

Cover design by Gary Swift

For Louis and Clara

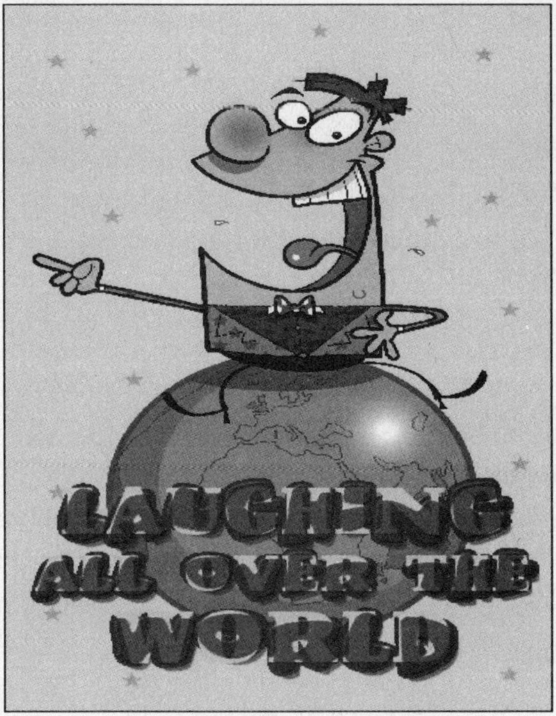
LAUGHING
ALL OVER THE
WORLD

Preface

India has the largest number of homeless and abandoned children in the world. Many of these children have to work and never get the chance to go to school. Furthermore, a large part of the population has limited access to medical treatment. Diseases which are preventable in western countries are rife in India and consequently many children die before the age of five.

For over ten years one charity has been working tirelessly to help provide a real home for children who have never known love, care and security in their lives. The Kings World Trust for Children works in Tamil Nadu in Southern India. It is not an institution, the children become part of a unique family committed to giving them a childhood and a sustainable future through education and training.

Kings World Trust for Children now has 180 children in residential care and supports many others in an 'outreach' care programme. Children with severe physical and mental disabilities are also supported by the Trust in a community programme. The Trust runs two rural health clinics and operates a Health Education Programme and HIV/AIDS awareness projects in 100 rural villages. The Trust was heavily involved in Tsunami relief and reconstruction projects and now runs a Youth Activities Centre for 500 children in one tsunami disaster village. Kings School provides an education in English for over 700 children, many of whom are orphaned, children with disabilities and bright children from low income families. The Trust's volunteer programme enables around 60 volunteers each year from UK, US and Europe, to work in India to support the Trust's projects.

In December 2004 the Indian Ocean earthquake and tsunami affected many millions and the people of Southern India and Tamil Nadu in particular were affected by the disaster. The Kings

World Trust was one of the first aid agencies on the spot with emergency aid.

Kings World Trust for Children is doing something positive to make a real difference to children in real need in a very poor part of South India. The results of their work will bring a sustainable future to many disadvantaged, marginalised and disabled children who would otherwise have had no future.

This Cartoon and Joke Book, with the support of so many people around the world, is a contribution to the work of this charity. All profits from the sale of this book will go to the Kings World Trust for Children, helping with the very special work of this unique charity in Southern India.

I wish this joke book every success and commend it to you.

Penelope Keith, OBE, DL
Patron
Kings World Trust for Children

Contents

Mother, you can put the
water back, I like it deep !

How do you communicate with a fish?
You drop him a line!
Anoushka age 10

What kind of fish purrs?
A cat fish!
Lauren age 9

Why do oysters never give to charity?
Because they are shellfish.
Lucy age 14

What's yellow and dangerous?
Shark infested custard!
Sebastian age 5

What do sharks eat?
Fish and ships.
John age 6

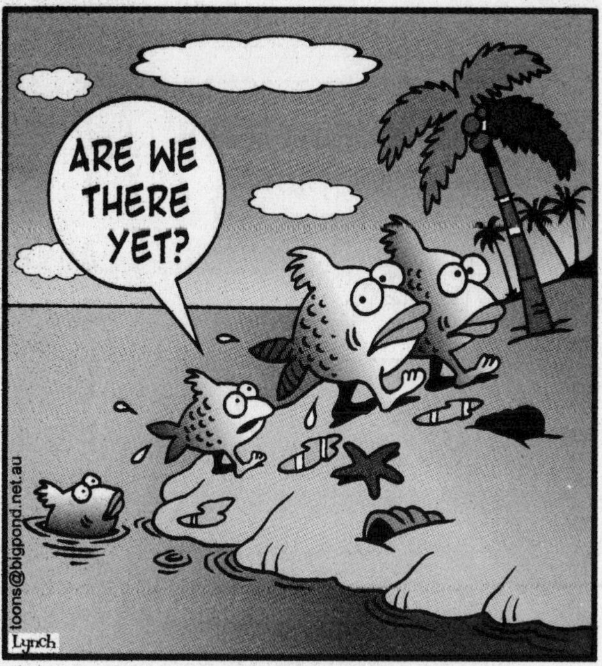
ARE WE THERE YET?
toons@bigpond.net.au
Lynch

How could the dolphin afford to buy a house?
He prawned everything.
Lauren age 9

What's a shark's favourite game?
Swallow the leader.
Jess age 9

What do you call a fish with no eyes?
A fsh.
Polly age 10

Why do seagulls fly over the sea?
Because if they flew over the bay they would be bagels.
Rose age 11

What happened to the shellfish when he
went to a seafood disco last week?
He pulled a muscle.
Verity age 9

Why are fish so clever?
Because they live in schools.
Ayomide age 11

What kind of fish goes best with ice-cream?
Jellyfish.
Ben age 9

Why are fish boots warm in the North Pole?
Because they have electric 'eels!
Jemima age 12

What kind of fish like icy conditions?
Skate.
Marcus age 9

What's the coldest fish in the ocean?
The Blue Whale.
Ross age 6

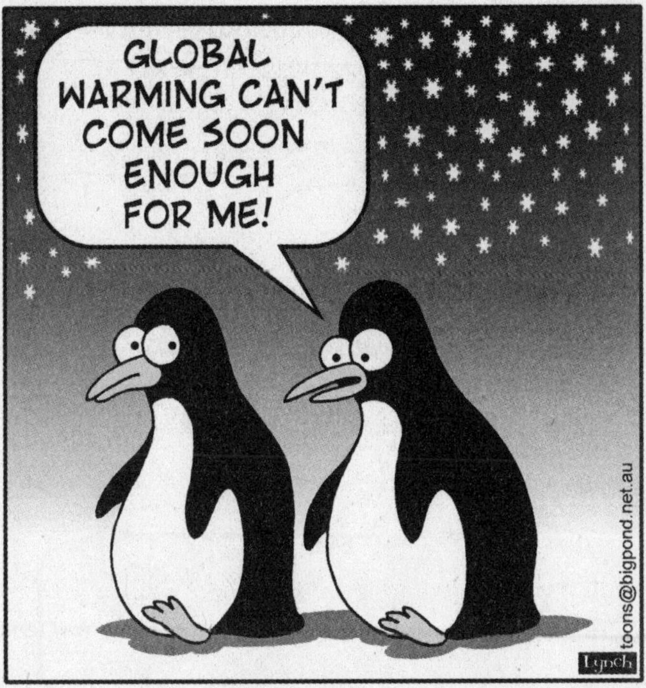
GLOBAL WARMING CAN'T COME SOON ENOUGH FOR ME!
toons@bigpond.net.au
Lynch

What is black and white and red all over?
A sunburnt penguin.
Evangeline age 9

What is black and white and goes round
and round and round and round....?
A penguin stuck in a revolving door.
Matthew age 10

What do you get if you cross a goldfish
with an ice cube?
A cold fish.
Greta age 9

"Hasn't our lad adapted well
to climate change?"

A man who owns a small budgerigar thinks that his bird is looking a bit lonely and so buys another budgie to keep it company. The next morning the man discovers the new bird lying dead at the bottom of the cage. Thinking this was unfortunate he buys another budgie but the same thing happens. The new bird is lying dead in the cage. Unperturbed by this misfortune he buys a parrot and puts it in the cage with the budgie.

There is quite a lot of squawking throughout the night and in the morning the parrot is dead at the bottom of the cage. After careful thought the man buys a bigger cage and a buzzard to keep his budgie company. Once again though he finds the new bird dead in the morning. Finally he buys a large sea eagle . The following morning the sea eagle is dead and the budgerigar has no feathers left. "Ha!" says the man to the budgie, "What happened this time?" "Well," says the budgie "I had to take my jacket off for that one!"

Andrew age 15

"They won't let anybody in!"

A man buys a parrot. When he gets home, all is well, except the parrot won't stop swearing obscenities at him. He gets so fed up that he decides to lock it away in the garden shed. This doesn't work and he can still hear the bird swearing from the house. So he brings it in and locks it in a cupboard – the bird just screams at him even more and the neighbours start to complain.

Next day his girlfriend is meant to be coming round, and as a last resort he stuffs the bird into the fridge. Miraculously the bird suddenly shuts up, so he takes it out and puts it back on its perch. All day the bird behaves perfectly and the man's girlfriend goes away really taken with it. So the man says to the parrot "Glad to see you have changed your ways at last!" "Yes," says the parrot, "I'm really, really sorry...please forgive me!" "OK," says the man, "just as long as you don't do it again!" "I won't" says the parrot, casting a nervous eye at the fridge. "By the way...What did the chicken do?"

Nick age 15

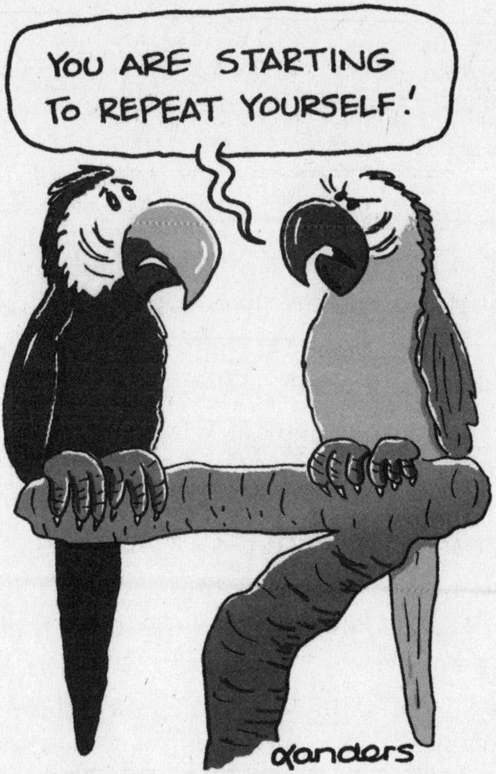
YOU ARE STARTING TO REPEAT YOURSELF!
Xanders

What do you call a lost parrot?
A polygon.
Rufus age 13

What is parrot food called?
Polyfilla.
Aravind age 15

What did the geese say when they
saw a duck flying over?
Duck.
Charlotte age 13

What bird is always out of breath?
A puffin.
Poppy age 14

What do you call a woodpecker with no beak?
A head banger.
Bert age 12

**Dave, please stop playing with
the children !**

What do you call a chicken
that eats cement?
A bricklayer.
Claudia age 7

What is the strongest bird in the whole world?
A crane.
Harry age 4

"I do wish you'd be a
more responsible parent!"

A duck goes into a butcher shop and asks, "Have you any peas?" the butcher says no. So the duck comes in the next day and asks again, "Have you any peas?" The butcher replies "No, but if you come in here and ask me if I have any peas tomorrow, I will nail your feet to the floor." The duck comes in again the following day and says "Have you any nails?" The butcher replies "No", so the duck says "Alright then have you got any peas?"
Cameron age 12

Why don't ducks tell jokes when they are flying?
Because they would quack up!
Dan age 11

A duck went shopping in a smart department store. He waddled up to the first floor and asked an assistant for a bright red lipstick.
"Certainly" she replied and went to look for one. She returned holding a very bright red lipstick which the duck liked.
"How would you like to pay?" the assistant asked.
The duck replied "Just put it on my bill."

Claire age 12

I didn't lay it !

Why did the chewing gum cross the road?
Because it was stuck on the chicken's foot.
Mitchell age 6

Why did the cockerel cross the road?
To show he wasn't a chicken!
Danny age 11

Why did the hen leap over the road?
She was a spring chicken.
Nina age 11

What do you call an Irish bird of prey that
hunts only at night, and enjoys
listening to New Romantic music?
O'Kestrel Manoeuvres in the Dark.
Tristan age 7

"Can you hear horses?"

A chicken walks into a public library, goes straight up to the desk and says in a rather chickeny way, "Book!" The librarian looks surprised but the chicken repeats the request "Book!" The librarian gives the chicken a book and off it goes contentedly. The following day the chicken returns, with the book, places it on the librarian's desk and once again says "Book!" The librarian gives the chicken a book and the chicken puts the book under its arm and waddles off.

The following day this is repeated. After a week the chicken is coming in and saying "Book! Book!" The librarian is giving the chicken two books each time. The librarian's curiosity gets the better of him, so one day he follows the chicken. The chicken goes out of the library, joins the towpath by the canal and heads out into the open country. After a mile or so the chicken arrives at a pond where there is a large frog sitting on a lily pad. The chicken holds up the first book. The frog looks at it and says "Rrrrredditt!!"

Andrew age 15

One day a man went to an auction. While there he decided to bid for an exotic parrot. He was really fascinated by this bird and was determined to buy him. He got caught up in the bidding but kept getting outbid, so he bid higher and higher and higher.

Finally after he bid far more than he had intended, he was the proud owner of the bird. As he was paying he asked the auctioneer "I really hope this parrot can talk. I have paid so much for him that I would be so disappointed if he was mute."

"Don't worry" said the auctioneer, "He can talk. Who do you think kept bidding against you?"

Maudie age 9

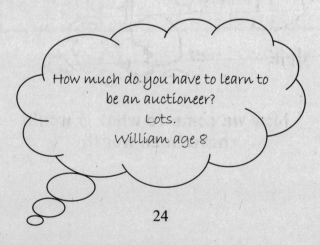

How much do you have to learn to be an auctioneer?
Lots.
William age 8

Now we come to what it would
have been worth

What do Chinese cats like to eat?
Egg fried mice
Imogen age 9

Why do cats chase birds?
For a lark.
Emily age 4

What do you call an accident-prone cat?
A catastrophe.
Lauren age 7

What do cats like to draw best?
Paw-traits.
Joshua age 5

What do you get if you cross a cat with a bat?
A cat flap.
Melissa age 3

" NO THANKS, TIDDLES.... I JUST HAD ONE."

There were two cats preparing to race across the Channel. The English cat was called "One two three," and the French cat was called
"Un deux trois". They dived in and started to swim. Who do you think won?
The English cat of course as Un deux trois quatre cinq! (cat sank)

William age 12

27

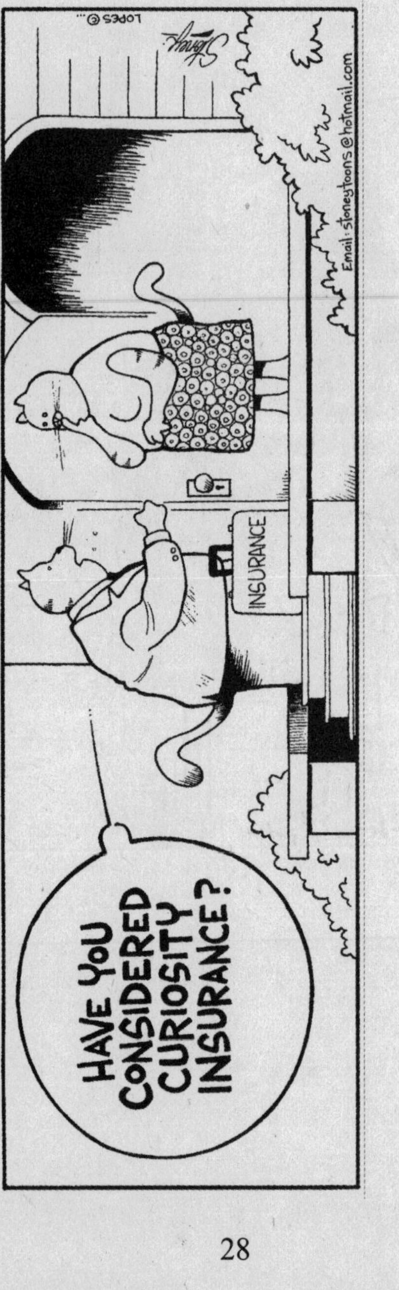
HAVE YOU CONSIDERED CURIOSITY INSURANCE?
INSURANCE
Email: stoneytoons@hotmail.com

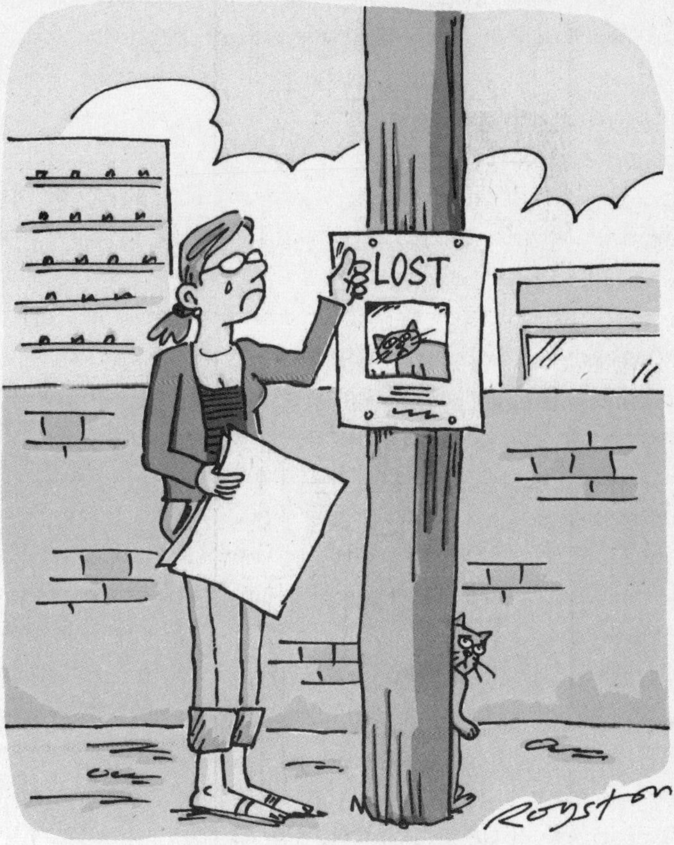
LOST
Royston

A local business was looking for office help. They put a sign in the window stating the following: "Help wanted. Must be able to type, must be good with a computer, and must be bilingual. We are an Equal Opportunity Employer."

A short time afterward, a cat trotted up to the window, saw the sign and went inside. He looked at the receptionist and purrs, then walked over to the sign, looked at it and meaowed.

Getting the idea, the receptionist got the office manager. The office manager looked at the cat and was surprised to say the least. However, the cat looked determined, so he lead him into the office. Inside, the cat jumped up on the chair and stared at the manager.

The manager said, "I can't hire you. The sign says you have to be able to type." The cat jumped down, went to the typewriter, and proceeded to type out a perfect letter. He took out the page and trotted over to the manager and gave it to him, then jumped back on the chair. The manager was stunned but then told the cat, "The sign says you have to be good with a computer."

The cat jumped down and went to the computer. The cat proceeded to enter and execute a perfect program that worked flawlessly the first time. By this time, the manager was totally dumbfounded.

He looked at the cat and said, "I realize that you are a highly intelligent cat and have some interesting abilities. However, I still can't give you the job."

The cat jumped down and went to a copy of the sign and put his paw on the sentence about being an Equal Opportunity Employer.

The manager said, "Yes, but the sign also says that you have to be bilingual." The cat looked at the manager calmly and said, "Woof!"
Chris age 12

Glenturret Distillery searching for new cat to replace Towser.

Strathearn Herald, April 05

What do you call a cat that has just
eaten a whole duck?
A duckfilledplattypuss!

Jessica age 10

32

What do you call platypi
wearing hats?
Platypi!

Chloe age 7

A man is exploring in the heart of Africa, battling his way through an area of tall grass when he chances upon a rather large lion standing in his path. Having been told that the best way to deal with this situation is simply to follow and imitate the lion's movements he gives the lion a hard stare and lowers his hands to the ground. The lion gently sits down on its hind legs; the man does the same, never losing eye contact with the lion. The lion lies down and gently brings its front paws together. The man does the same. After a few moments the lion says to the man, "I don't know what you're doing but I'm saying grace!"
Andrew age 15

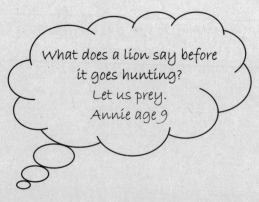

What does a lion say before it goes hunting?
Let us prey.
Annie age 9

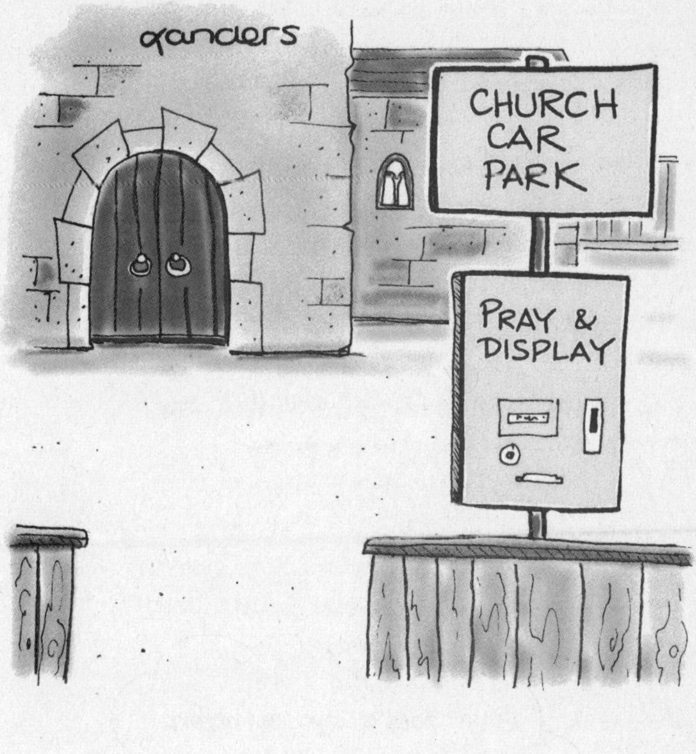

qanders
CHURCH
CAR
PARK
PRAY &
DISPLAY

What is the difference between a wet day
and a lion with toothache?
One pours with rain and the other
roars with pain.
Isobel age 9

What's a crocodile's favourite game?
Snap.
Lulu age 6

A man walks into a bar with a lion and
asks the bartender,
"Do you serve zookeepers?"
The bartender replies "Of course, we serve everyone here."
The man says "Then, I would like to order a pineapple
juice and a zookeeper for my lion!"
Sosie age 9

What do you call a horse sunbathing
behind railings?
A zebra.
Claudia age 7

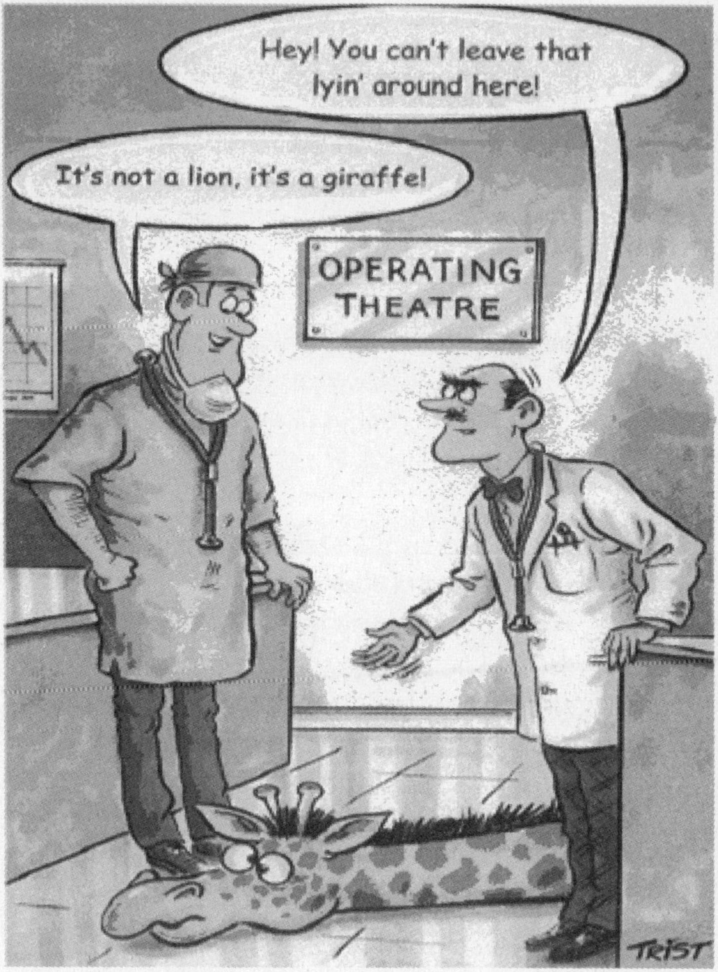
Hey! You can't leave that lyin' around here!
It's not a lion, it's a giraffe!
OPERATING THEATRE
TRIST

Why didn't the rhino's mobile work?
He had forgotten to charge it.
Charlie age 4

What has two tails, five ears and
two horns?
A rhino with spare parts.
Ian age 7

How do you know if there is a rhino
in your bedroom?
You can't shut the door.
Phoebe age 4

What do you call a camel with three
humps?
Humphrey.
Louis age 12

What do you get if you cross a giraffe with a
hedgehog?
A five metre hairbrush.
Josie age 7

"How come you can always get a signal?"

What has six legs, four ears and stripes?
Someone riding a zebra.
Sophie age 6

If a dictionary goes from A to Z
What goes from Z to A?
A Zebra.
Marcus age 9

What's white, fluffy and swings through the jungle?
A Meringue-u-tang.
Harry age 11

Who are the most famous reptile movie stars?
Darth Gator and Jimmy Newt-tron.
Evan age 9

While sports fishing off the Darwin coast, a tourist's boat capsized. Although he could swim, his fear of crocodiles kept him clinging to the capsized craft. Finally spotting a beachcomber on the shore, he shouted out to him, "Hey, are there any crocodiles around here?"

"No," the man yelled back. "There haven't been any crocs 'round these parts for years!"

Feeling more at ease, the tourist started swimming leisurely towards shore. When he was about halfway there, he shouted out to the beachcomber again, "How did you get rid of the crocs?"

"Oh, we didn't do anything'," the beachcomber yelled back. "The sharks got every last one of them!"

James age 11

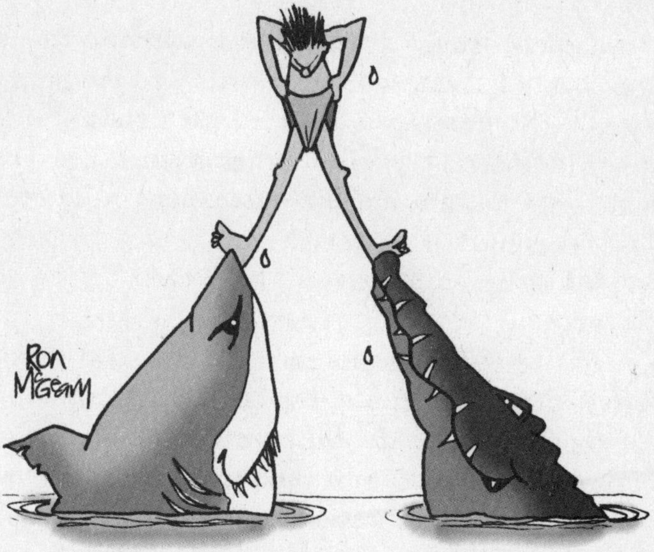
Ron McGeary

A policeman stops a car that's swerving around crazily, and is amazed to see that in the back there are six penguins flapping around. "What's going on?" he says to the driver. The driver replies "Well, I've just won these six penguins in a raffle, and I haven't a clue what to do with them!" "If I were you I'd take them to the zoo" suggests the cop.

Next day he sees the same car, still swerving around. When he stops it, the penguins are flapping about even more excitedly – but now they are wearing sunglasses. "I thought I told you to take them to the zoo yesterday!" he exclaims. "I did" answers the driver, "and they enjoyed themselves so much I'm taking them to the beach today!"

Nick age 15

"You know that's not what I meant
when I asked you to take the dog out!"

My dog had a gammy eye so I took him to the vet who held him in his arms, looked into its eyes looked back at me and said, 'I'm sorry, I'm going to have to put your dog down'.

'Why? Because he's got a gammy eye?'

"No, because he's REALLY heavy!"

Dom Wood

What happens when you cross a gun dog with a telephone?

You get a Golden Receiver.

Jessica age 10

What do you call a puppy that chews everything?

Very gnaw-ty.

Clara age 10

What do you call a dog that likes travelling the world?

A jet-setter.

Paul age 9

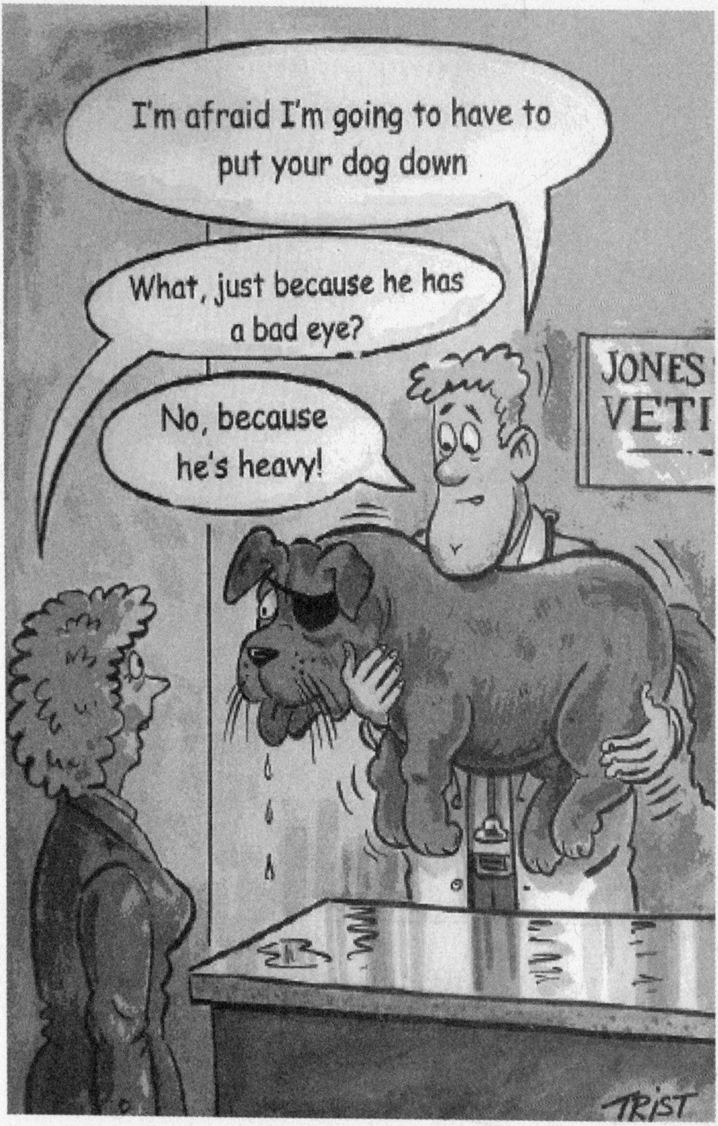
I'm afraid I'm going to have to put your dog down
What, just because he has a bad eye?
No, because he's heavy!
JONES
VETI
TRIST

Ibrahim: "I have lost my pet dog."
Irfan: "Don't worry! Advertise in the newspaper."
Ibrahim: "Oh! But my dog can't read!"
Shanmugapriya age 11

My dog's got no nose.
How does he smell?
Awful!
Imogen age 8

Why don't dogs make good dancers?
Because they have two left feet.
Jessica age 10

What do you call an alcoholic dog?
A whino.
Jessica age 10

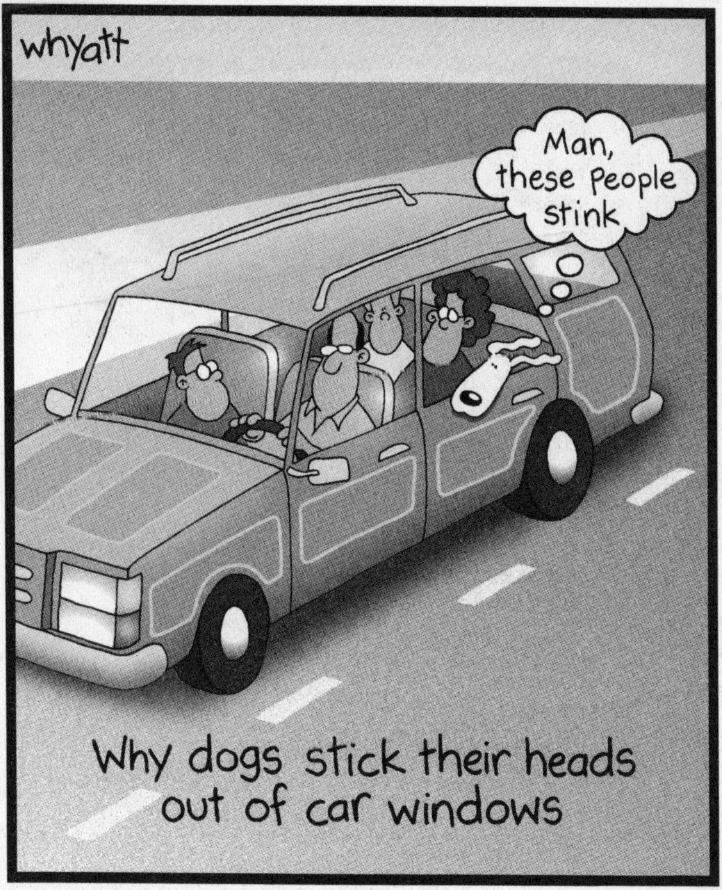
whyatt
Man, these people stink
Why dogs stick their heads out of car windows

NOW THATS WHAT I CALL A GOATEE BEARD!

A man visits a farm and sees a three-legged sheep. He tells the farmer "you must really love your animals to keep a disabled sheep like that."

The farmer smiles, "Well," he says, "she is a show sheep and won many a prize for me in her time, plus when my daughter fell into the lake and nearly drowned, the sheep jumped in and saved her life!"
The visitor was most impressed. "And so is that how she lost her leg?"

"No," replies the farmer, "but you don't eat a sheep like that all at once."

Eliza age 12

50

What do you call a deer with no eyes?
No-eye-deer!
Sebastian age 5

What do you call a deer with no eyes and no legs?
Still no idea.
Edmund age 9

What's got four legs and goes 'Boo'?
A cow with a cold.
Nick age 15

What's white and wooly and goes 'AAAAH'?
A sheep with no lips.
Nick age 15

Where do cows go on Saturdays?
To the MOOvies.
Hettie age 13

One sunny day a farmer was milking his cow, when a fly flew into the shed. It buzzed around the farmer's head, then flew straight into the cow's ear. A few minutes later the farmer looked down to see the fly swimming in the pail of milk. "Just look at that," he exclaimed" it must have gone in one ear and out the udder!"

Freddie age 8

What do you call a bull asleep on a road?
A bulldozer!
Tom age 7

What do you get if you push a cow forwards?
A pat on the head.
Mungo age 9

Cows

About

Talking

Idiot

This

With

Stuck

Been

I've

Long

How

Look

1. Tell them to say cow before each word.
2. Say cow after each word.
3. Say cow before and after the words.
4. Read from the bottom up.

Danny age 11

54

The Bear Essentials — by Steve Midgley

There were two twin baby skunks, and one of them was named "In" and the other one was named "Out".

They used to play all day, but never together. Whenever In played inside, Out played outside, and whenever Out was out, In was in - if you see what I mean, but although they were absolutely identical, their Mother always knew whether it was In who was in, or Out who was out, or in fact, whether it was Out who was in, or In who was in fact out!

When asked how she could tell, she merely said: "Instinct"!!!
Olivia age 11

What do you do if you get eaten by an elephant?
Run around and around and around until you're all
pooped out.
Webb age 5

Why were the elephants banned from
the swimming pool?
Because they wouldn't keep their trunks up!
James age 10

What do you call an elephant that can't do sums?
Dumbo.
Anoushka age 10

Why did the elephant spit the clown out?
He tasted funny.
George age 6

What do polar bears have for lunch?
Ice burgers!
William age 10

What do you call an elephant at the north pole?
Lost.
Anoushka age 10

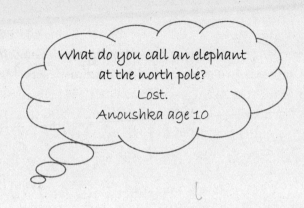

What did the man say when he saw four elephants
coming over the hill?
"I see four elephants coming over the hill."
What did the man say when he saw four elephants
coming over the hill, wearing dark glasses?
Nothing, he didn't recognise them.
Benjamin age 6

What do you call an elephant that never washes?
A smellyphant!
Imogen age 8

Why are elephants wrinkled all over?
Because they don't fit on an ironing board.
Imogen age 8

What's small, grey and has a trunk?
A mouse going on holiday!
Henry age 11

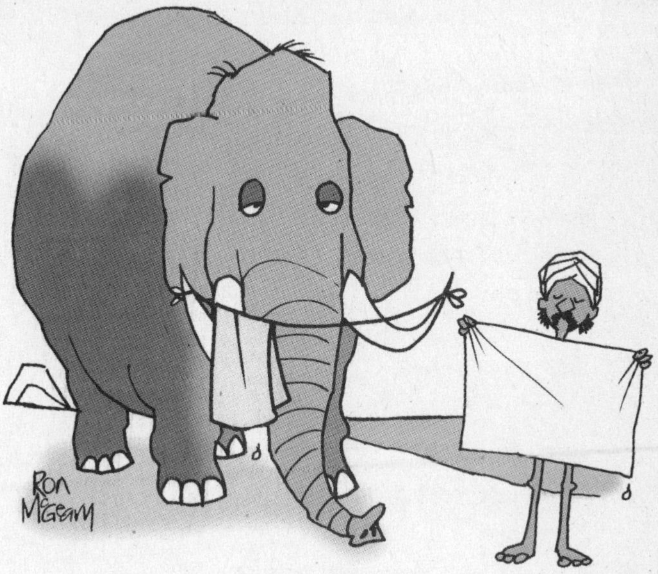
Ron McGeary

What do you call a dinosaur with one eye?
A do-you-think-he-saur-us!
Olivia age 8

How do dinosaurs pass exams?
With extinction.
Freddie age 11

How do you fit six donkeys in a police car?
Two in the front, three in the back,
and one on the top, going "eeh-awh, eeeh-awh."
Lily age 9

What do you call a donkey with only three legs?
Wonky.
Richard age 10

What did the beaver say when he swam into the wall?
Dam.
Sasha age 14

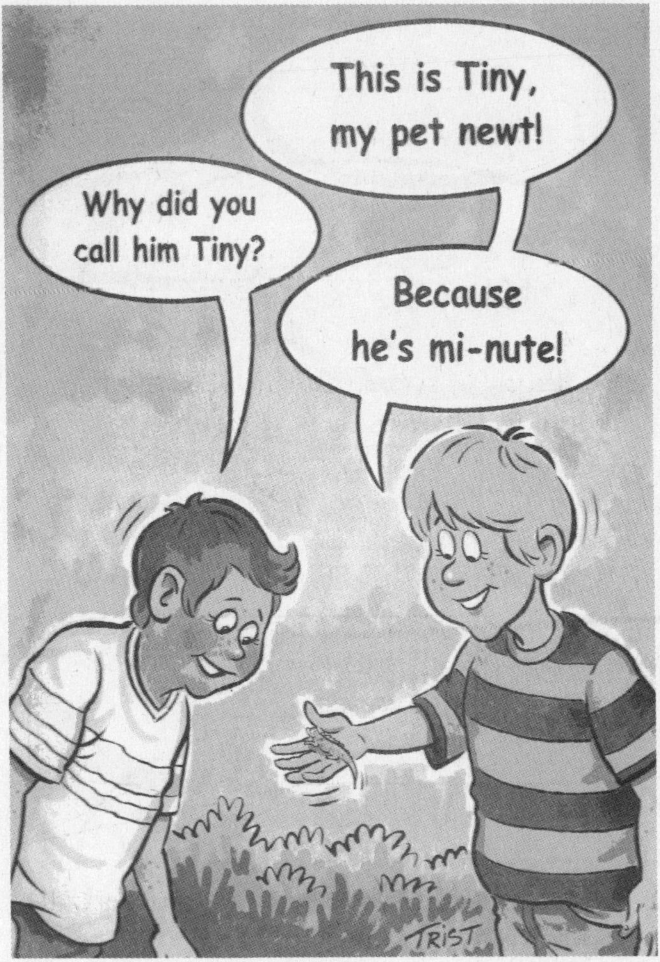
This is Tiny,
my pet newt!
Why did you
call him Tiny?
Because
he's mi-nute!
TRIST

There are two turtles sitting in a tank.
One says to another: "Well do you know how to drive this thing?"
Nick age 15

Why did the turtle cross the road?
To get to the Shell station.
Anna age 14

What's the difference between a coyote and a flea?
One howls on the prairie, the other prowls on the hairy.
Tabitha age 2

How do snails keep their shells clean?
Snail varnish.
Benjamin age 6

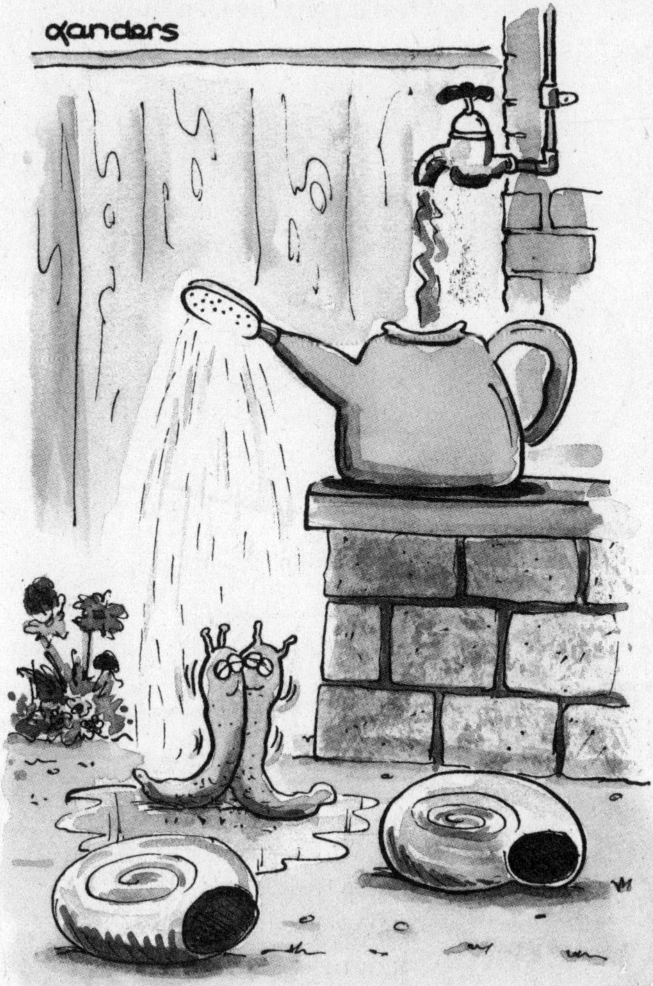
Xanders

What do you call a snail?
A slug with a crash helmet!"
Maharaja age 12

What's the definition of a slug?
A homeless snail.
Gus age 11

"Well for a gastropod like Sidney, foot and mouth disease is about as bad as it gets"

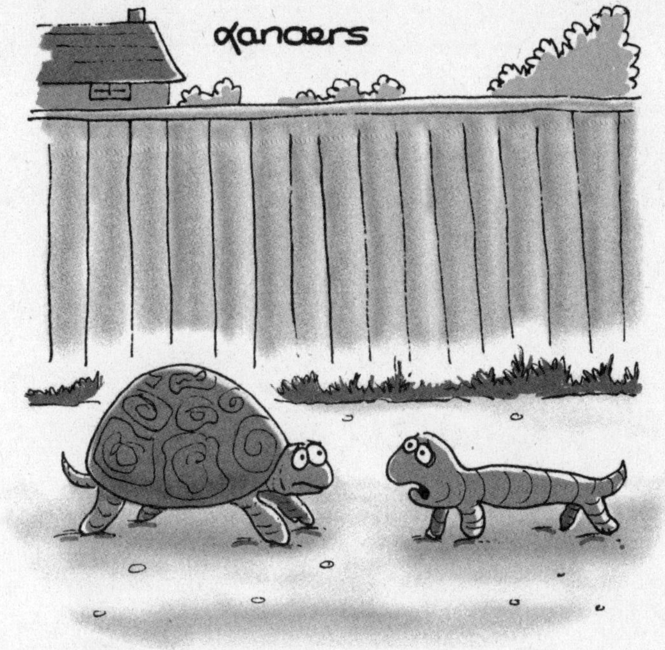
Xanders

I've been evicted !

What goes ninety-nine donk, ninety-nine donk?
A centipede with a wooden leg.
Jasmine age 8

What did the ear wig say when
it fell off the cliff?
Ear we Go!
Alex age 7

Why do bees have sticky spiky hair?
Because they use honeycomb.
Frankie age 10

What do butterflies rest their heads
on when they sleep?
Caterpillows.
Lucy age 5

"IT'S NO GOOD, I CAN'T GET UP - I'M ON MY LAST LEGS!"

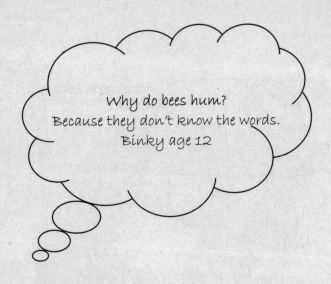

Why do bees hum?
Because they don't know the words.
Binky age 12

On a dark evening a man was walking home when he met an enormous, gross, ugly cockroach. Before he could react the cockroach punched and then fled. The man's face was really bruised and started to swell up so his wife took him to casualty.

The doctor asked "How did you get such bruises?" The man looked at him and said   "Well this will sound very strange but a great big ugly cockroach thumped me." The Doctor replied: "Oh I had realized there was a nasty bug going round."

Sean age 14

I THINK YOU HAVE PICKED UP A BUG!
DOCTOR
Xanders

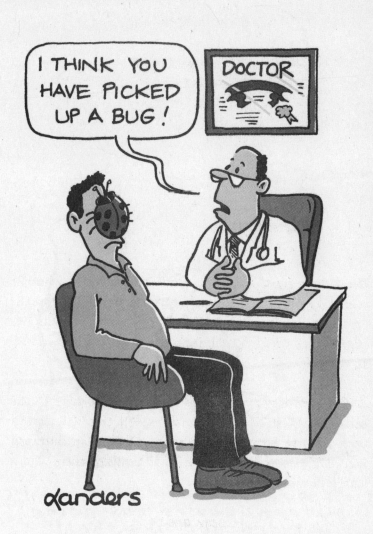

Why are snakes clever?
Because you can't pull their leg?
Julia age 10

What do you get when you cross a snake with a porcupine?
Barbed wire!
Alec age 9

"I don't care if you are sixteen. You're not going out dressed like that!"

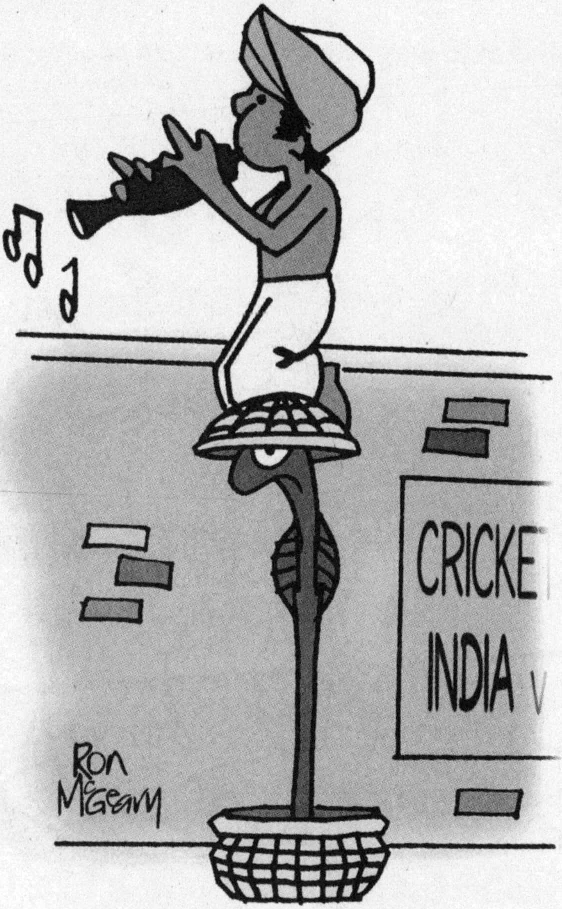
CRICKE
INDIA V
Ron McGeary

What's a hare's favourite dance?
Hip-hop
Alex age 11

What do you call a man covered in rabbits?
Warren.

A man was driving in his car, when he ran over a rabbit. He felt so awful, so he got out of his car and knelt beside the rabbit. He wondered what to do to help it, but just then a woman drove up in a mini. She took out a bottle and put some of the liquid that was in it onto the rabbit. This had a dramatic effect and it started to hop around, and finally hopped away. The man was amazed and asked, "What did you put on that rabbit?" The woman read the bottle and said: Hare restorer. Restores dull and lifeless hare.

Sophia age 9

WAITER! THERE'S A HARE IN MY SOUP!

What do you call a long line of still hamsters?
A hamsterjam.
Zoe age 6

Spell mousetrap in only three letters.
CAT.
Lulu age 6

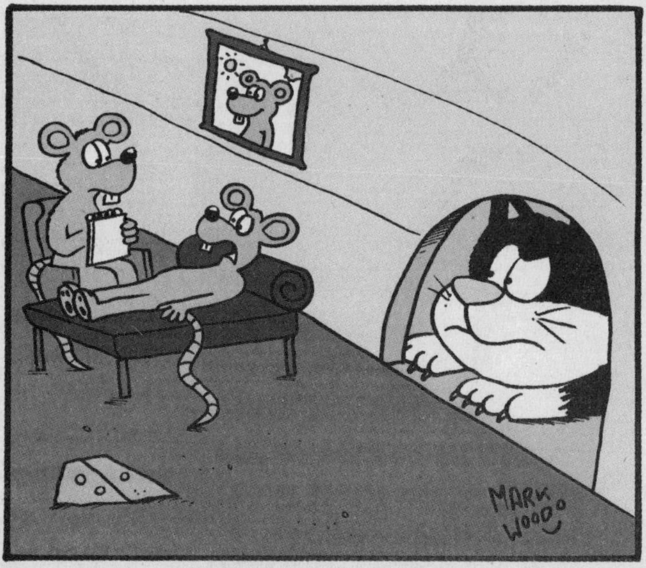
MARK WOOD

"I FEEL TRAPPED!"

Hamster joyriders!

What do you call it when
two hamsters almost collide?
A narrow squeak.
Clara age 10

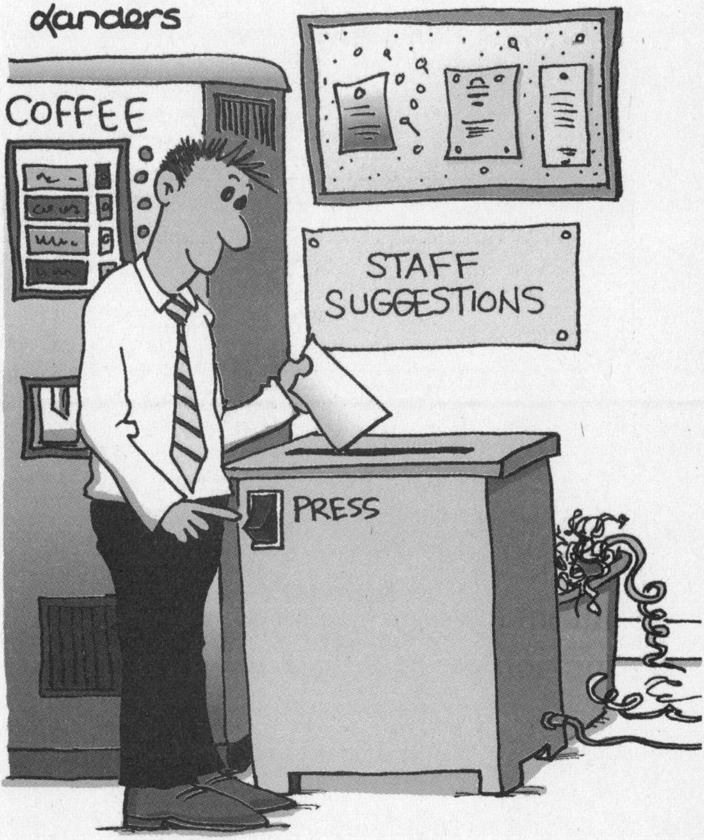

Xanders
COFFEE
STAFF SUGGESTIONS
PRESS

A boy came to school with a swollen nose.
The teacher asked "How did that happen?"
"I was smelling a brose" the boy said woefully.
"I think you mean a rose" replied the teacher "as there is
no B in rose"
"There was in this one" said the boy.
Clementine age 10

Why is Cyclops such a good teacher?
He only has one pupil!
Flora age 9

Why did the jellybean go to school?
Because he wanted to become a Smartie!
Dylan age 10

Why did the Headmaster marry the cleaner?
Because she swept him off his feet!
Clara age 10

Kate Taylor

Teacher: "You missed school yesterday didn't you?"
Pupil: "Not very much!"
Radha age 13

"I'm not going to school today," Alexander said to his
mother. "The teachers bully me and the boys in my
class don't like me."
"You are going. And that's final. I'll give you two good
reasons why."
"Why?"
"Firstly, you're 35 years old.
Secondly, you're the headmaster!"
Sasha age 6

'But how can you blame my parents because I'm the worst pupil in your school, when YOU are my father?'

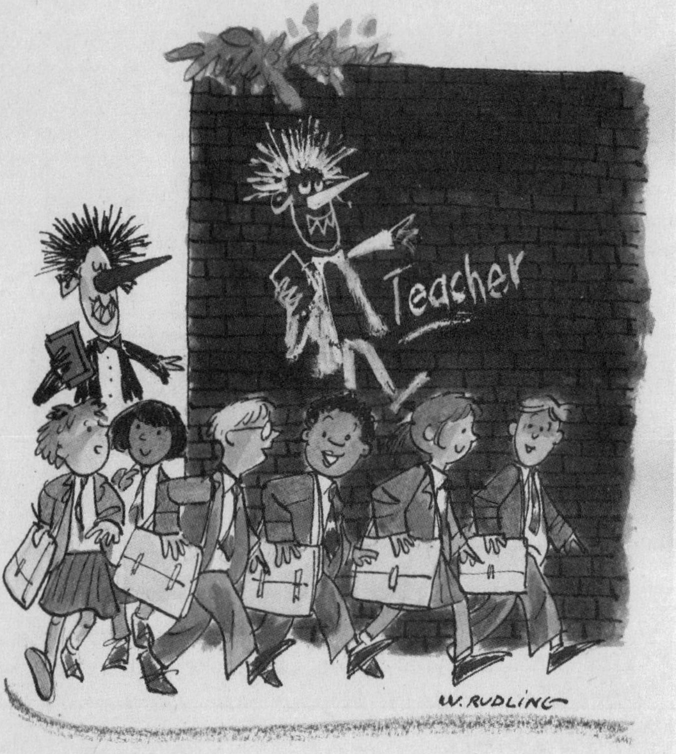
Teacher
W. RUDLING

"Please sir, there was a frog in Michael's lunch."
"Tell Michael to speak to me himself," replied the teacher.
The boy explained "Sorry sir, he's got the frog in his throat!"
Cassie age 9

What kind of food do Maths teachers eat?
Square meals.
Ross age 12

Why did the boy eat his homework?
His teacher said it was a piece of cake.
Paige age 13

What subject do runners like best?
Jog-raphy.
Amy age 12

Steve Breen, San Diego Union-Tribune

Teacher: "Tell me your tables, John."
John: "Dining-room table, kitchen table,
bedside table...."
Sasha age 6

What's one and one? Two
What's four minus two? Two
Who wrote Tom Sawyer? Twain
Now say all the answers together.
Two, two, twain
Have a nice twip!
Richard age 12

Teacher: "Sharmila, what is the formula for water?"
Sharmila: "H,I,J,K,L,M,N,O"
Teacher: "What are you saying?"
Sharmila: "Yesterday you said that the formula for water is H to O"
A. Anushiya age 11

Please sir! Please sir!
Why do you keep me locked up in this cage?
Because you are the teacher's pet.
Jasmine age 8

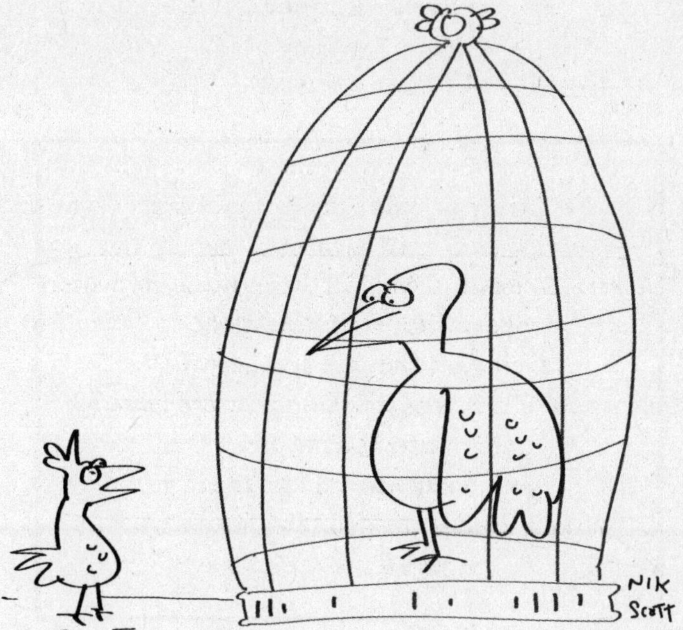
NIK
SCOTT

What are you in for ?

Daughter: "I'm tired of doing my homework."
Father: "Come on now, homework never killed anyone."
Daughter: "I know, but I don't want to be the first."
Katherine age 15

A little girl came home from school
and said to her mother
"Mummy, today I was punished
for something I did not do."
The mother exclaimed
"But that is terrible. I am going to have a
talk with your teacher about this....
by the way, what was it that you didn't do?"
The little girl replied "my homework."
A Preethi age 12

What do elves do after school?
Gnomework.
Maddie age 14

Please Sir, a virus ate my homework....

What was the Maths book explaining
to the French text book?
I have so many problems.
Arun age 11

Why was the number 6 afraid?
Because 7 8 9.
Kirstie age 9

Why is it dangerous to do any maths in the jungle?
Because if you add 4 and 4 you get 8.
Clara age 10

What goes ha ha thud?
A man laughing his head off.
George age 14

Did you know there are 12 seconds in a year?
The second of January, the second of February....
Imogen age 8

"The Head will see you now."

© Royston

Which State is the cleverest in America?
Alabama because it has 4 a's and 1 b.
Kelly age 11

What has 4 eyes but no face?
Mississippi.
Derek age 11

"Did you know that eight out of ten school
children use pencils to write with?"
"Gosh! What do the other two use them for?"
Sasha age 6

What did one pen say to the other pen,
when they were about to start a fight?
Draw!
Jemima age 13

What did one pencil say to the other pencil?
Take me to your ruler.
Emily age 13

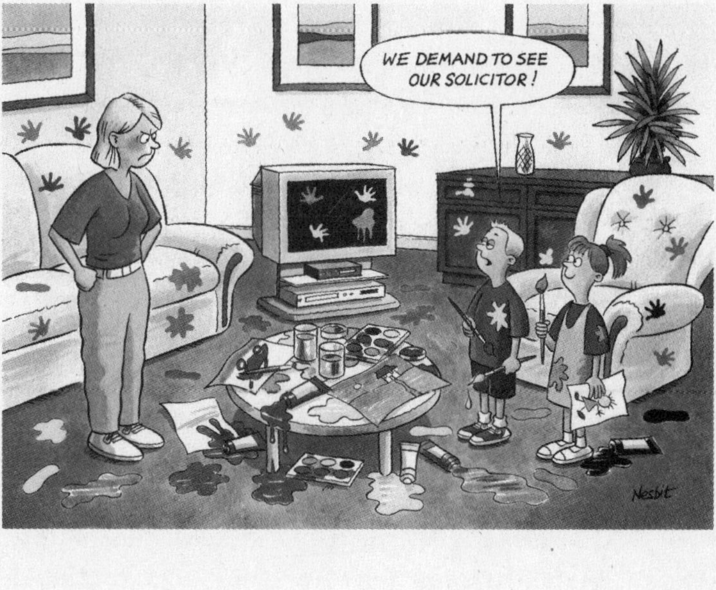
WE DEMAND TO SEE OUR SOLICITOR!
Nesbit

There was a young boy whose teacher told him to learn the first 3 letters of the alphabet. So he went home and asked his mum "What's the first letter of the alphabet?" His Mum replied, "Bog off you little twit, can't you see I'm busy".

So he went to his sister and asked her, "What's the second letter of the alphabet?" She was watching the lottery results and said, "two thousand, six hundred and seventy eight – 2678". So off he goes to see his brother who is watching Noddy. He asked him "What's the third letter of the alphabet?" The brother replied, "in my little broom-broom car."

The next day at school, the teacher asked him if he learnt what the first three letters of the alphabet were.

He said "Bog off you little twit, can't you see I'm busy". The teacher was furious and said, "how many detentions do you think you are going to get for this?"

"2678" he replied. The teacher goes on to say "How do you think you will get away with this?"
He said, "In my little broom-broom car!"

Ibby age 9

"WAIT TILL YOUR FATHER
GETS BACK FROM
PARENTING CLASS."

What is a forum?
Two-um plus two-um.
Tom age 7

Why did the teacher wear sunglasses?
Because her pupils were so bright!
Rosie age 9

Why did the teacher turn on the lights?
Because her pupils were so dim.
Rosie age 9

'I suppose that makes YOU top of the class . . .'

Why did everybody want to
hang out with the mushroom?
Because he was a fungi, (fun guy).
Rachel age 13

What did the banana do when
he was late for school?
He split.
Arun age 11

"WELL, HOW DID LITTLE MISS JONES GET ON
WITH HER NEW KINDERGARDEN CLASS?"

What kind of fish do you call
when your piano needs fixing?
A tuna fish
Alexander age 6

"Haven't I seen your face before?" a judge demanded,
looking down at the defendant.
"You have, Your Honour," the man answered hopefully.
"I gave your daughter violin lessons last winter."
"Ah yes," recalled the judge. "Twenty years!"
Barney age 11

Why did the pianist always bang his
head on the keys?
He was playing by ear.
Alastair age 12

How does the music teacher reach
the highest notes?
He climbs up a ladder.
Oliver age 5

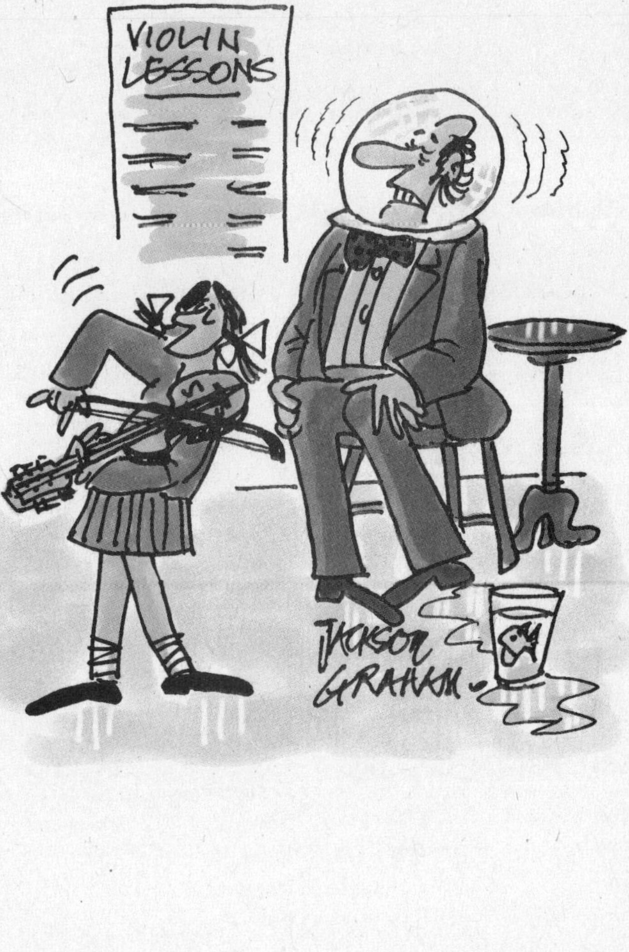
VIOLIN
LESSONS
JACKSON
GRAHAM

The insects were having their annual cricket match.
The captain was a Grasshopper, who turned to the
Cricket and said, "Are you a bowler?"
"Of course," said the Cricket.
"Who ever heard of a cricket bat?"
Max age 8

At one point during a game, the coach said to one of his young players, "Do you understand what cooperation is? What a team is?"

The little boy nodded yes.

"Do you understand that what matters is whether we win together as a team?"

The little boy nodded yes.

"So," the coach continued, "when you are called out, you don't argue or attack the umpire. Do you understand all that?"

Again the little boy nodded.

"Good," said the coach, "now go over there and explain it to your mother."

Carl aged 12

The Packers and Bears (rival American football teams. Packers are from Wisconsin and Bears are from Illinois) were having an ice fishing contest. The Packers were hauling in fish after fish and the Bears were having no luck. Finally the Bears sent over a spy to see what the Packers' trick was. He came running back and exclaimed, "They're cheating! They're drilling holes in the ice!"

Aaron age 14

"I've got something to tell you Dad - I don't like fish...I mean I REALLY don't like fish...I HATE fish Dad. There, I've said it now"

Why did the basketball court get wet?
The players dribbled.
Matt age 9

Why did the bicycle not win the race?
He got two tyred.
Poppy age 14

Finally reaching the top of a steep hill,
the two men on a tandem bicycle
were panting and sweating profusely.
"Wow, that was a tough climb," said the driver in front.
"Wasn't it," replied the second chap.
"I am so glad I kept the brake on or
else we would have slid down backwards."
Adam age 11

I phoned the local gym and I asked if they
could teach me how to do the splits.
He said, "How flexible are you?"
I said, "I can't make Tuesdays or Thursdays."
Rob age 14

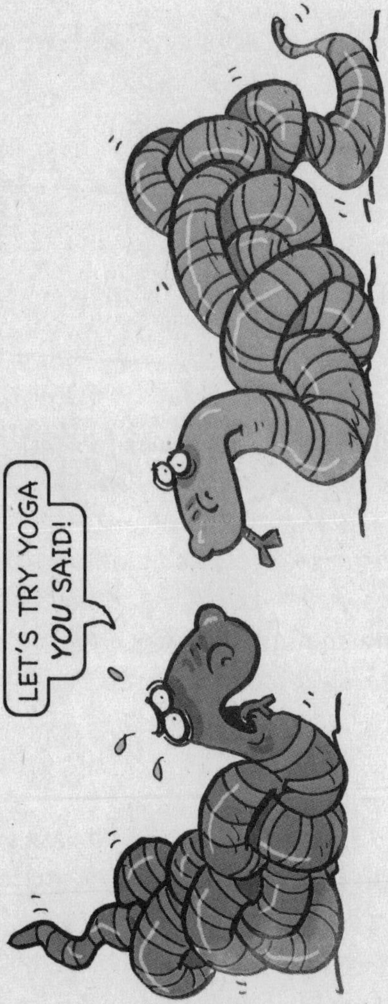
LET'S TRY YOGA YOU SAID!

"Have you got any Monsters' ink?"

What happens when a ghost gets lost in the fog?
He's mist.
Amelia age 6

What do you say to a two-headed monster?
Hello, hello!
Phoebe age 3

What drink do ghouls like best?
Lemon and slime!
Edmund age 4

Who does a ghoul marry?
His ghoulfriend!
Patrick age 2

What does a monster do when he loses a hand?
He goes to a second hand shop!
Isabella age 4

Why did the boastful ghost take off?
He was full of hot air.
Clara age 10

What room does a ghost go to keep alive?
The living room.
Charles age 11

Why do actors avoid ghosts?
They don't want to get stage fright.
Helen age 7

Why do ghosts like to take lifts?
It raises their spirits.
Charlie age 4

What do ghosts like to eat?
Ghoulash.
Pippa age 9

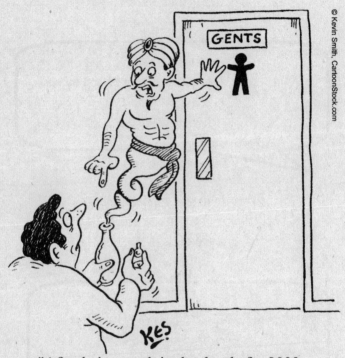

"After being stuck in that bottle for 2000 years, I have to do something urgently before I can start granting you wishes!"

What do you get if you cross a
skeleton with a detective?
Sherlock Bones.
William age 8

Why was the skeleton so scared?
He had no guts.
Charlie age 3

Why do skeletons drink milk?
Because it's good for the bones.
Alexander age 4

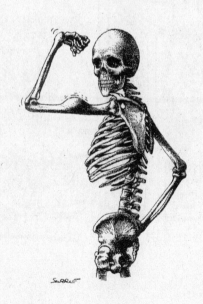

What is Dracula's favourite pudding?
I scream.
Lutanga age 12

What do you get when you cross a
snowman with a vampire?
Frostbite.
Derek age 11

What is a vampire's favourite ice cream?
Vein-illa.
Jessica age 10

Did you hear about the stupid
vampire who listened to a match?
He burnt his ear.
Jasmine age 8

What does a vampire do with only one fang?
He grins and bares it.
George age 6

What did the toothless vampire say?
Fangs aren't what they used to be.
Belinda age 6

What type of blood does a vampire have?
Donated.
Rachel age 13

Two vampire bats wake up in the middle of the night, thirsty for blood. One says, "let's fly out of the cave and get some blood."

"We're new here," says the second one. "It's dark out, and we don't know where to look. We'd better wait until the other bats go with us."

The first bat replies, "Who needs them? I can find some blood somewhere." He flies out of the cave.

When he returns, he is covered with blood.

The second bat says excitedly,
"Where did you get the blood?"

The first bat takes his friend to the mouth of the cave.

Pointing into the night, he asks,
"See that black building over there?"

"Yes," the other bat answers.

"Well," says the first bat, "I didn't."

Ellie age 12

How does a bat fly without bumping into things?
He uses wing mirrors.
Oliver age 5

I THINK TODAY'S GONNA BE ONE OF
THOSE DAYS, BATMAN!

What do you call a wizard from outer space?
A flying sorcerer.
Jasmine age 8

What kind of star goes to jail?
A shooting star.
Glenna age 14

Why did the witch put her broom
in the washing machine?
She wanted a clean sweep.
Jasmine age 8

What do you call two witches who share a room?
Broom-mates.
Jasmine age 8

What do you call a motorbike belonging to a witch?
A broom stick.
Alexander age 4

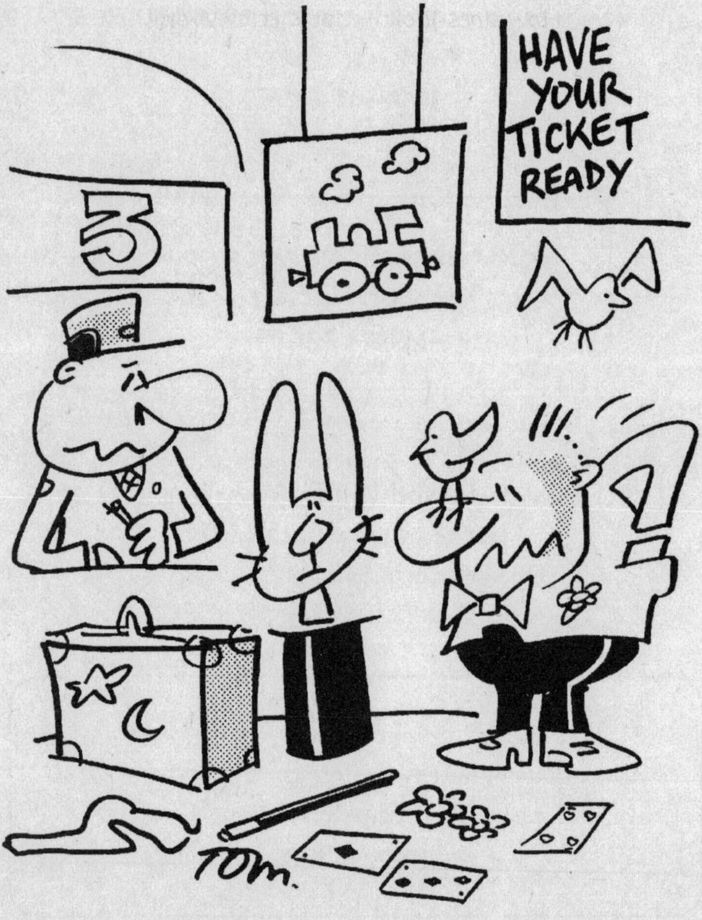
HAVE YOUR TICKET READY
3
TOM.

How does Jack Frost Get to Work?
By icicle.
Jasmine age 8

Why do witches think they're funny?
Every time they look in the mirror it cracks up!
Verity age 9

What subject do all witches do best at school?
Spell-ing!
Verity age 9

What did the monster eat after
getting its tooth pulled?
The dentist.
Jimmy age 3

What game do little monsters like to play?
Hide and shriek.
Harry age 4

Why did the champion monster give up boxing?
He did not want to spoil his looks.
Sasha age 6

A man was walking home to his house down a quiet suburban street. As he walked along the pavement, suddenly he could hear behind him this loud knocking. He looked behind and saw a coffin thumping down the street behind him. A shiver ran down his back and he started walking faster, but when he turned round the coffin was still behind him. He started jogging slightly but still the coffin was coming closer and closer. He started running but the coffin was faster, thumping behind.

Thankfully he reached his house, jumped the gate and opened his front door. By now the coffin was almost on his back. He rushed up the stairs of his house, the coffin following him. Panting, he ran into the bathroom, slammed the door and the coffin was coming up the stairs.

In a panic, he opened the bathroom cupboard, gulped down some cough medicine and the coffin stopped.

Charlie age 12

What did the cobra say to the ghost player?
Charmed to meet you.
Hugo age 6

What do you get if you cross a snake with a witch?
Abra-da-cobra.
Sam age 9

Why are snakes so good at spells?
Because they remember all the hisss tory.
Meredith age 9

Why did the snake say his mouth hurt?
He had a fork in his tongue.
Neil age 11

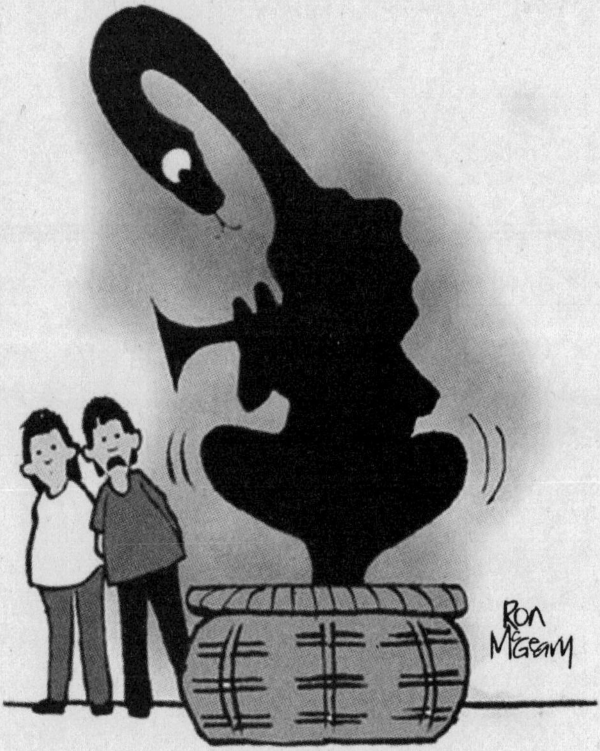
Ron McGeary

Doctor, I keep seeing spots before my eyes!

"Doctor, Doctor, I keep feeling I'm a goat."
"How long have you had this feeling?"
"Since I was a kid."
Tim Brooke-Taylor

"Doctor, Doctor, everyone keeps ignoring me."
"Next Please!"
Holly age 10

"Doctor, Doctor, I keep shrinking."
"Please be patient."
Anna age 11

"Doctor, Doctor I feel like a rubber band."
"Please stretch out and tell me all about it."
Esme age 7

Doctor: "Please call a doctor immediately.
I have got severe stomach-ache"
Helper: "Sir, you are a doctor yourself.
Why do you need to call another doctor?"
Doctor: "Because my fees are too high!"
Esther age 10

"Doctor, Doctor, I feel like a pair of curtains."
"Well pull yourself together then."
Holly age 10

"Doctor, Doctor, you have to help me out."
"Of course, which way did you come in?"
Michael age 9

"Doctor, Doctor, I feel like a spoon."
"Well sit still and don't stir."
Bridie age 5

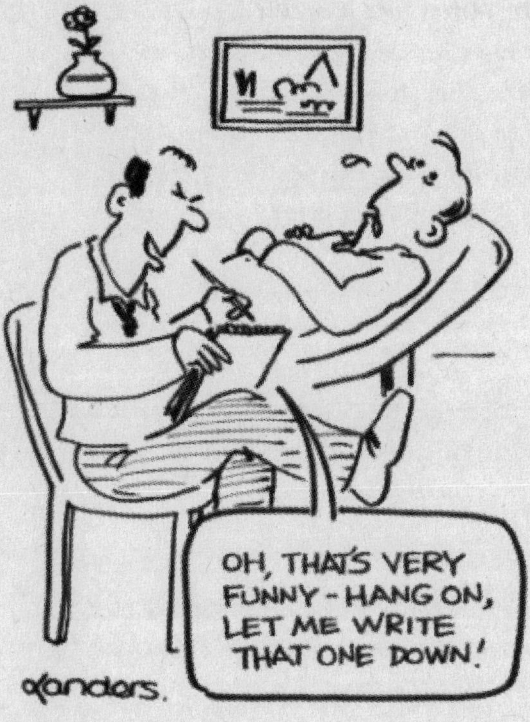
OH, THAT'S VERY FUNNY - HANG ON, LET ME WRITE THAT ONE DOWN!
Xanders.

"Doctor, Doctor, I feel like a needle."
"I do see your point."
Lulu age 6

"Doctor, Doctor, I think I'm a bridge.."
"What came over you?"
"A bus and three cars."
Rosie age 9

Why did the banana go to the doctor?
Because he was not peeling very well.
Lucy age 7

A wolf goes to the doctor,
"Doctor, Doctor, I feel like a Granny".
"Are you feeling old?"
"No, just hungry!"
Clara age 10

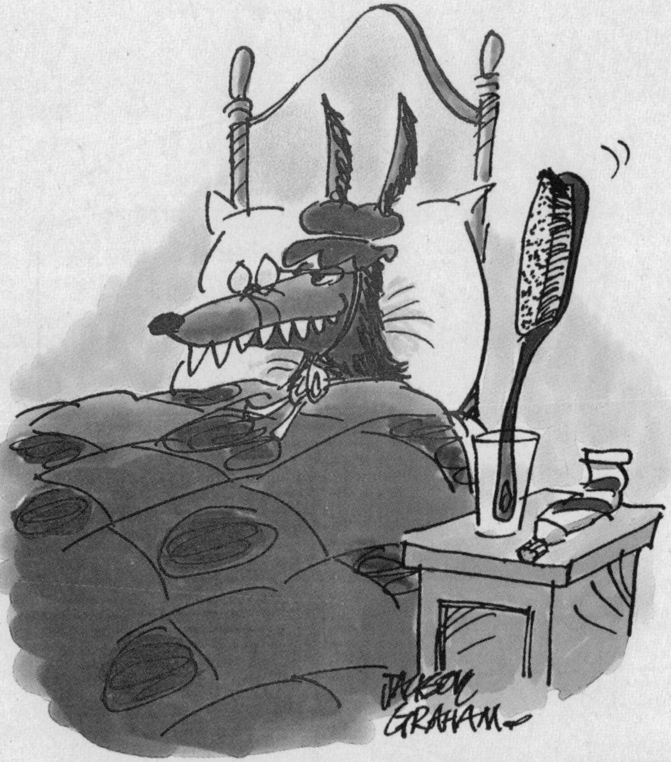
GRAHAM

"Doctor, Doctor, I keep seeing double."
"Take a seat, please."
"Which one?"
Sasha age 6

"Doctor, Doctor, I feel like I've got
a strawberry growing out of my head."
"I'll give you some cream for that!"
Holly age 10

"Doctor, Doctor, I feel like a horse."
"Well your condition seems stable."
Simon age 8

What kind of bandage do people
wear after heart surgery?
Ticker Tape.
Sasha age 6

"Doctor, Doctor, I keep thinking I'm a door!"
"You're just a little unhinged."

Why did the boy sneak past the medicine cabinet?
He didn't want to wake the sleeping pills.
Anna age 14

What did one eye say to the other eye?
Just between you and me, there is something that
smells!
Robin age 10

Why did the head chase his body?
He wanted to get ahead.
Tom age 7

Where do you take a sick horse?
A horse-pital.
Verity age 9

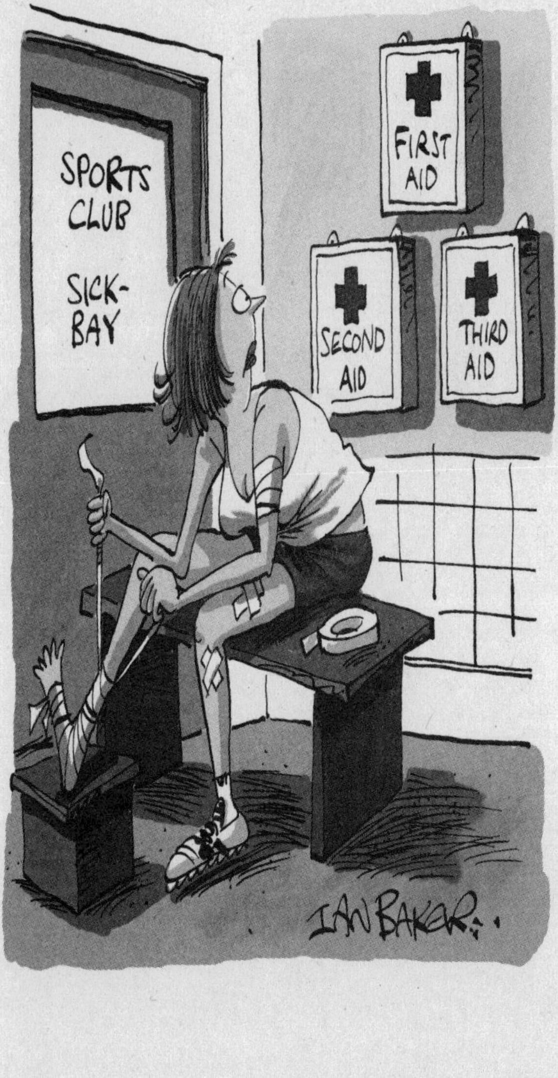
SPORTS
CLUB
SICK-
BAY
FIRST
AID
SECOND
AID
THIRD
AID
IAN BAKER

What's red and silly?
A blood clot.
Stephen Fry

"No wonder Daddy's exhausted-he's been watching the Marathon!"

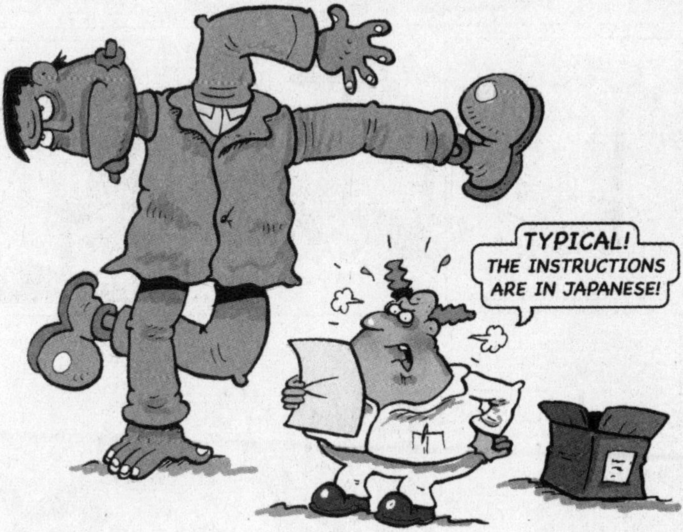
TYPICAL!
THE INSTRUCTIONS ARE IN JAPANESE!

What do you call a boomerang that doesn't come back?
A stick
Rowan age 15

What do you call a Frenchman in sandals?
Phillipe Flop
NIAMH CUSACK

Why do the French only give one egg at Easter?
Because one is un oeuf (enough).
Louis age 12

How do the Egyptians ring a doorbell?
Toot and come in (Tutankhamen).
Sophia age 7

Why was the Egyptian boy confused?
Because his Daddy was a Mummy.
Ivo age 8

Who is the Pharoah's favourite chef?
Gordon Ramses
Lara age 9

Did you hear about the man who
jumped off the Eiffel Tower?
Apparently, he was in Seine.
Thomas age 8

What do you call an Italian with a rubber toe?
Roberto.
Chloe age 3

What does a Spanish farmer say to his hens?
Ole!
Louis age 12

What do you call two Spanish firemen?
Jose A and Jose B.
Thomas age 2

What do you call a Spanish footballer with no legs?
A grassy arse (gracias)
Mark age 13

"I warned you not to throw in
our old holiday currency."

What do you call a robbery in Beijing?
A Chinese takeaway!
George age 11

What do you call a Chinese woman
with a food mixer on her head?
Blenda!
Sebastian age 5

What country do bees like to visit?
Stingapore.
Louis age 12

What's the fastest food in the world?
scone   (s'gone)....
Charles age 13

What do you call someone who opens
an Indian restaurant in Buenos Aires?
An Argie Bharji!
Tom age 12

" NOW LET ME GET THIS STRAIGHT BEFORE YOU STARTED KILLING EACH OTHER, HE FLICKED A SPOONFUL OF HOT CHOP SUEY AT YOU , THEN YOU FLICKED HIM WITH A SPOONFUL OF CURRY AT HIM. "

Some English sailors were sailing off the German
coast. Their boat began to sink.
"Mayday, mayday, We are sinking !"
The reply came back "Vat are you sinking about?"
Ian age 11

What's an Irishman's most famous invention?
A floating anchor!
Fergus age 11

How do you sink an Irish submarine?
Knock on the door and wait for them to open it.
How do you sink the same submarine again?
Knock on the door and wait for them to open the
window and say "We're not falling for that one again".
Jamie age 14

My dad used to be in the Navy. He was in the
Submarine Service. He was kicked out because he was
caught sleeping with the windows open!
Nicky age 10

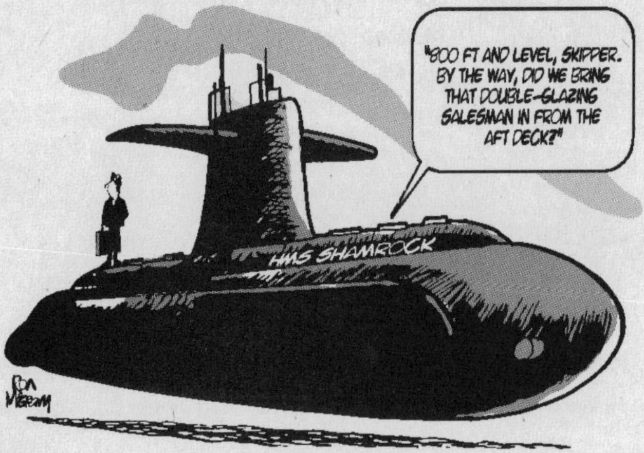
"800 FT AND LEVEL, SKIPPER. BY THE WAY, DID WE BRING THAT DOUBLE-GLAZING SALESMAN IN FROM THE AFT DECK?"
HMS SHAMROCK

What do you call a cat who walked
across the desert?
Sandy Claws.
Paige age 13

What do you call a snowman in the desert?
A wet patch in the sand.
Julia age 9

An American pilot was flying over the Australian
outback when his plane malfunctioned and plummeted
to the ground. When the pilot awoke, he found himself
in bed, in an Australian hospital.
"So," he asked the doctor, "Did I come here to die?'
"No," the doctor said. "You came here yesterday."
Sebastian age 9

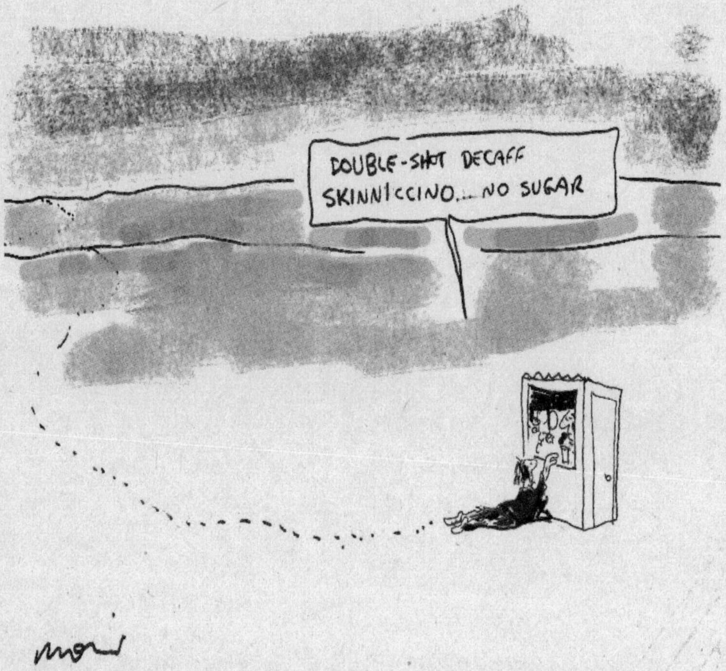
DOUBLE-SHOT DECAFF
SKINNICCINO... NO SUGAR

What stays in one place but travels around the world?
A stamp.
Olivia age 7

There was an English man, Irish man, and Scottish man all having a race, when suddenly they get to a fence. So the English man says, "I will get over the English way." So he chops down a tree and puts two logs on each side and jumps over the fence. The Irish man says, "I will get over the Irish way." So he gets some pliers and clips a hole through the fence and runs through the hole. The Scot says, "I will get over the Scottish way." So he puts one leg over the fence but gets stuck and says "Eek I kee me don't likey I got butty stuck on spikee!"
Freddie age 12

An Englishman, an Irishman, Scottish man, Welsh man, a Priest and a Monk, walked into a bar.
The barman asked: "Is this some kind of a joke?"
Guy age 11

How do you confuse an Irishman?
You put him in a round room and tell him there is a £10 note in the corner!
Fergus age 11

"Honey, remember yesterday when you had
your toe stuck, in the tap?"

There were three foreigners in England who could not speak a word of English, but they looked for work in the city. One found a job in an opera house, another found a job in a restaurant and the third found a job in a sweet shop. The person at the opera house learns to say "Mimi, Mimi",
the one at the restaurant learns to say
"knives and forks, knives and forks"
and the third one learns to say
"goodie goodie gumdrops, goodie goodie gumdrops".
One night they meet up near where a man has been killed. The police came along and questioned them. The policeman says to the first man,
"Who killed this person?" The first man replied
"Mimi, mimi".
The policeman asks the second man "What did you kill him with?"
The second man replies "Knives and forks, knives and forks".
The policeman then says "I will take you all to jail where you will be charged with the killing of this person".
The third man replies, "Goodie, goodie, gumdrops, goodie, goodie, gumdrops!"

Ivo age 8

Y'KNOW I RECKON THE SYSTEM DOES WORK!

A pilot coming into land at the airport asks the air traffic controller if he has permission to land. The controller says sure, but tell me your height and position.

The pilot replies "I'm about 5'4" and I am sitting at the front of the plane."

Anoushka age 10

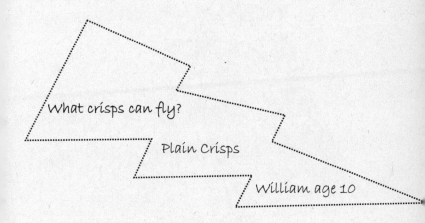

What crisps can fly?

Plain Crisps

William age 10

Deacon

A young guy called Kenny, moved to Texas and bought a donkey from a farmer for $100. The farmer agreed to deliver the donkey the next day.

The following day the farmer drove up and said 'Sorry son, but I have some bad news, the donkey died."

Kenny replied "Well then, just give me my money back."

The farmer shook his head and said "I can't do that. I went and spent it already". Kenny said, "OK, then, just bring me the dead donkey." The farmer asked, "What ya gonna do with him?" Kenny said, "I'm going to raffle him off."

The farmer said "You can't raffle off a dead donkey!" Kenny said, "Sure I can. Watch me. I just won't tell anyone he is dead."

A month later, the farmer met up with Kenny and asked, "What happened with that dead donkey?"

Kenny said, "I raffled him off. I sold 500 tickets at two dollars a piece and made a profit of $998."

The farmer was amazed, "Didn't anyone complain?"

Kenny said, "Just the guy who won. So I gave him his two dollars back."

Hector age 10

Why isn't a nose 12 inches long?
Because then it would be a foot.
Caleb age 14

An estate agent had just closed his first deal, only to discover that the piece of land he had sold was completely under water.
"That customer will be furious," he said to his boss. "Should I give him his money back?"
"Money back?" roared the boss. "What kind of salesman are you?
Get out there and sell him a houseboat!"
Andrea age 14

Mrs. Green lives in a green house. Mrs. Pink lives in a pink house. Mrs. Yellow lives in a yellow house. Who lives in the white house?
The President!
Nyla age 11

"It's perfect! I'll take it!"

STAINLESS
06

157

"WILL SOMEBODY SHOW THAT IDIOT HOW TO PLAY THE DIDGERIDOO"!

So I met this bloke with a didgeridoo and he was
playing Dancing Queen on it.
I thought that's Aboriginal.
Rob age 14

A British scientist and a Czechoslovakian scientist had spent their lives studying the grizzly bear. Each year they petitioned their respective governments to allow them to go to Yellowstone to study the bears. Finally their request was granted, and they immediately flew to New York and then on to Yellowstone. They reported to the ranger station and were told that it was the grizzly mating season and it was too dangerous to go out and study the animals. They pleaded that this was their only chance, and finally the ranger relented. The Brit and the Czech were given mobile phones and told to report in every day. For several days they called in, and then nothing was heard from the two scientists. The rangers mounted a search party and found the camp completely ravaged, with no sign of the missing men. They followed the trail of a male and a female bear. They found the female and decided they must kill the animal to find out if she had eaten the scientists because they feared an international incident. They killed the female animal and opened the stomach to find the remains of the Brit. One ranger turned to the other and said, "you know what this means don't you?" The other ranger responded, "Of course, the Czech is in the male."

Miles age 13

"I put it to the accused that he killed his victim with his bear hands"

How do you kill a circus?
Go for the Juggler!
Sara Cox

Why did the cassowary spit the clown out?
He tasted funny.
Imelda age 10

Why did everyone listen to the seven foot two
Norwegian?
He told tall stories.
Jorge age 11

*"No boys, I'm not a famous basket ball
player-guess again!"*

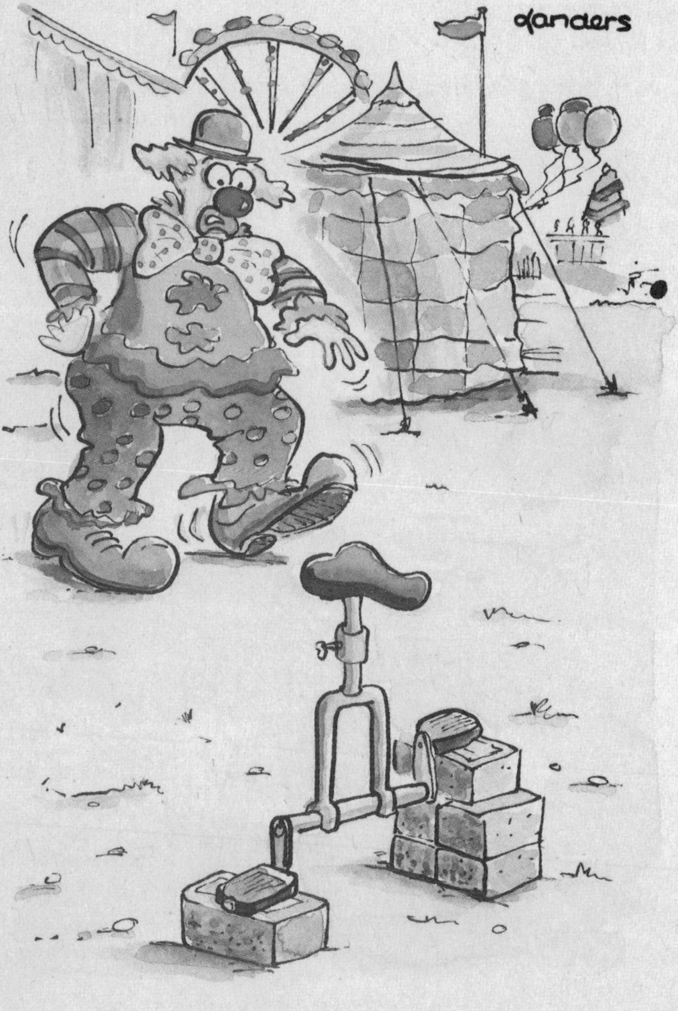
Xanders

A cowboy walks into a bar. The place is empty. He orders a beer.

The bartender brings it to him and the cowboy asks, "Where is everybody?"

The bartender says, "Gone to the hanging."

The cowboy says, "Hanging? Who are they hanging?"

Bartender says, "Brown Paper Pete."

"That's an unusual name," says the cowboy.

"We call him that because he wears a brown paper hat, a brown paper shirt, brown paper trousers and brown paper boots."

"That's weird!" says the cowboy. "What are they hanging him for?"

"Rustlin," says the bartender.

Annie age 16

A snail was in France, and went to a Land Rover dealer. He said that he wanted to buy a four-wheel drive, and he wanted a very large letter "S" on each door. He also wanted an "S" on the bonnet and the boot. The dealer did this, and the snail bought the car. He zoomed out of the dealership, and some Americans saw him speeding up the road. One of the Americans said to the other, "Man, look at that S-CAR GO!" ("escargot.")

Nick age 9

163

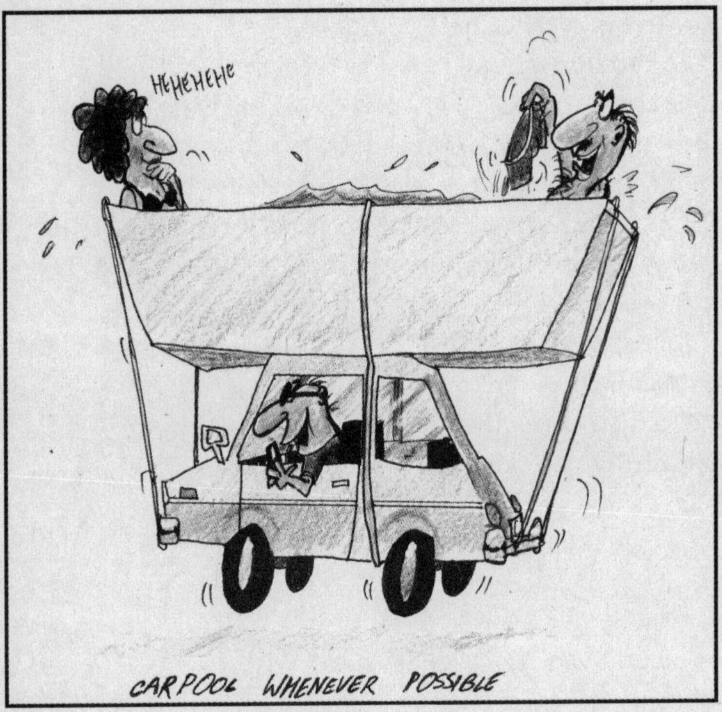
HEHEHEHE

CARPOOL WHENEVER POSSIBLE

"THERE MUST BE AN EASIER WAY TO MAKE THEM MOVE THAN GETTING THEM TO CHASE A STICK!"

Knock, Knock!
Who's there?
Tish.
Tish who?
Bless You.
Alice age 6

Knock, Knock!
Who's there?
Europe.
Europe who?
Europe to no good.
Alex age 10

Knock, Knock!
Who's there?
Isabelle.
Isabelle who?
Isabelle really needed on my bike?
Jess age 9

166

Knock Knock!
Who's there?
Alaska.
Alaska who?
Alaska you a question later.
Fred age 9

Knock, Knock!
Who's there?
Hawaii.
Hawaii who?
I'm fine thank you, Hawaii you?
Gregg age 6

Knock, Knock!
Who's there?
Snow.
Snow who?
Snow use, I've forgotten my key again.
Kasha age 11

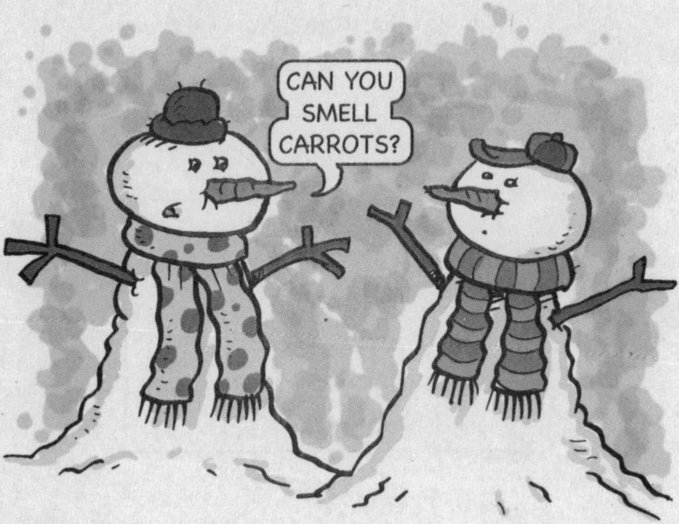
CAN YOU
SMELL
CARROTS?

Knock, Knock!
Who's there?
Boo.
Boo who?
Don't cry.
Caz age 16

Knock knock!
Who's there?
Francis.
Francis Who?
Francis a country in Europe.
Jasmine age 8

Knock, Knock!
Who's there?
Lettuce.
Lettuce who?
Lettuce in or we'll break the door down!
Jamie age 13

"Lucky your window was open, Mr. Smiff-and do you realise your tube's gone?"

Knock, Knock!
Who's there?
Harry.
Harry who?
Harry up and let me in!
Harry age 4

Knock, Knock!
Will you remember me in a day?
Yes.
Will you remember me in a week?
Yes.
Will you remember me in a month?
Yes.
Will you remember me in a year?
Yes.
Knock, Knock!
Who's there?
Have you forgotten me already!
Richard age 6

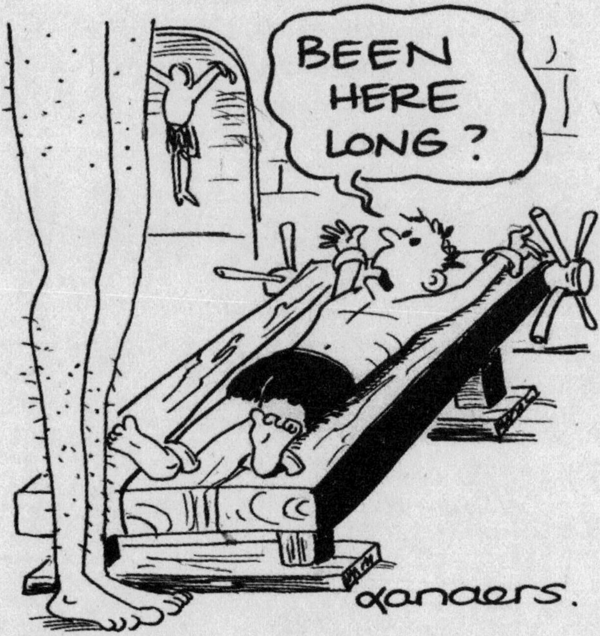
BEEN HERE LONG ?
Kanders.

Knock, Knock!
Who's there?
Nana.
Nana who?
That nana of your business.
Daisy age 8

Knock, Knock!
Who's there?
Cook.
Cook who?
That's the first cuckoo I have heard this year.
Neil age 8

Knock, Knock!
Who's there?
My dose.
My dose who?
My dose is duck id your ledderbox
Ian age 7

THESE DAYS YOU NEED THE BLOCKBUSTER PRODUCTION
TO DRAW THE PUNTER.

Knock, Knock!
Who's there?
Eddie.
Eddie who?
Eddie body home?
Edward age 8

Knock, Knock!
Who's there?
Oscar.
Oscar who?
Oscar a silly question, get a silly answer.
Lulu age 6

Knock, Knock!
Who's there?
Says.
Says who?
Says me, that's who!
Charlotte age 1

Dad: "Oh no, I just drove through a red light!"
Daughter: "Don't worry Dad, the Police car behind you
did exactly the same thing!"
Nicky age 10

Knock, Knock!
Who's there?
Police.
Police who?
Police stop making such a noise.
Robert age 6

Knock, Knock!
Who's There?
Irish Stew.
Irish Stew who?
Irish Stew in the name of the law!
Gus age 6.

What is the best address for a policeman?
999, Letsby Avenue.
Louis age 12

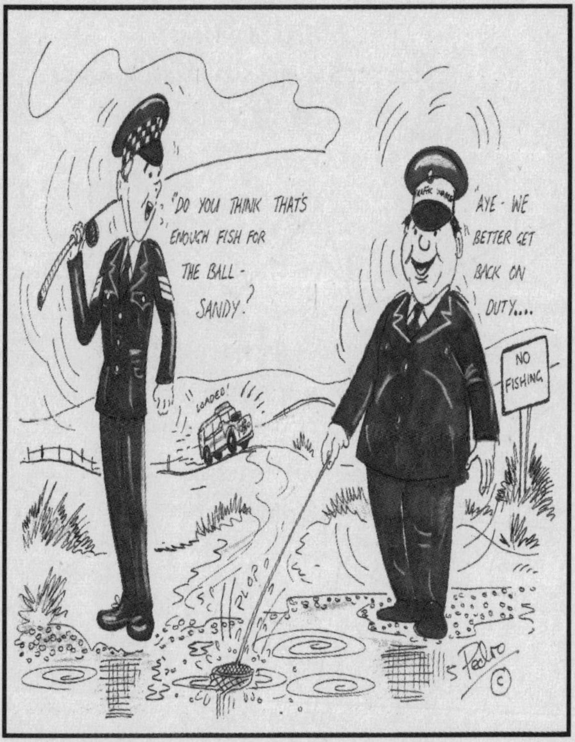
"DO YOU THINK THAT'S ENOUGH FISH FOR THE BALL - SANDY?"
"AYE - WE BETTER GET BACK ON DUTY....
NO FISHING
LOADED!
PLOP
Pedro ©

There were three robbers who were stealing from a factory. A policeman came into the building and heard a commotion. The robbers quickly jumped into some sacks and hid. The policeman kicked the first sack and the robber said "Meow" so the policeman, thinking it was a cat inside the bag, carried on searching the building. He then kicked the second sack and from inside the sack came the sound "Woof, woof" so the policeman carried on searching until he found a third sack. He kicked the sack. From inside the sack came the sound "Potatoes."

Hector age 10

"TERRIBLY SORRY. THOUGHT
SOMEONE SHOUTED WADER"

Waiter : Yes sir?
Customer: What soup is this?
Waiter : It's bean soup sir.
Customer: What?
Waiter : It's bean soup sir.
Customer : I don't care what it's BEEN
I want to know what it IS?
Richard Briers

Did you order the Leek soup?

Man to waiter: "A pork chop, please, and make it lean."
Waiter: "Certainly Mr. Smith, which way?"
Dylan age 10

"Waiter, waiter, have you got frogs' legs?"
"No sir, I always walk like this."
Sasha age 6

How did the glass feel when it was dropped?
Shattered.
Clara age 10

"I hear the dog food is good."

Why did the hamburger win the race?
Because it is fast food
Gemma age 9

What's worse than finding a slug
in your salad sandwich?
Finding half a slug!
James age 11

Another heavy lunch?

Why did the jello jiggle?
Because it saw the milk shake.
Maddie age 14

What do you call cheese that's not yours?
Nacho Cheese.
Rachel age 13

Two biscuits were crossing the road, when one got hurt.
What did the other biscuit say?
Crumbs.
Lily age 13

Why did the orange stop rolling down the hill?
It ran out of juice.
Jasmine age 8

Why didn't the banana snore?
Because it didn't want to wake up the rest of the bunch!
William age 10

What is yellow and points north?
A magnetic banana.
Adriana age 12

" NO SIR, THAT'S NOT PART OF THE INTERIOR DECOR —
IT'S THE MENU."

There were 3 men, an Englishman, an Australian and a Frenchman. They had to compose a sentence with the following 3 colours – yellow, green and pink.

The Englishman said, "When I woke up this morning I saw the yellow sun, a green apple and a pink flower".

Well done!

The Australian said, "When I woke up this morning I saw a yellow banana, the green grass and a lovely pink dress."

Well done!

The Frenchman said, "When I woke up this morning I heard the phone go GREEN GREEN, I PINK it up and say 'YELLOW'."

Jenny age 9

A coach driver is driving with a coach load of retired people when he is tapped on the shoulder by a little old lady. She offers him a handful of peanuts, so he thanks her, takes them, and gratefully munches them as he drives. After about 15 minutes, she taps him on the shoulder again and gives him another handful of peanuts. Again he thanks her, takes them and eats them up. This happens about five more times on the journey. Eventually, when she is about to hand him yet another handful, he asks the little old lady:

"Why don't you eat the peanuts yourself?"

"I can't chew them as I have no teeth" she replies.

The driver is puzzled.

"So why do you buy them, then?" he asks.

The old lady grins "because I just love the chocolate around them".

Albert age 6

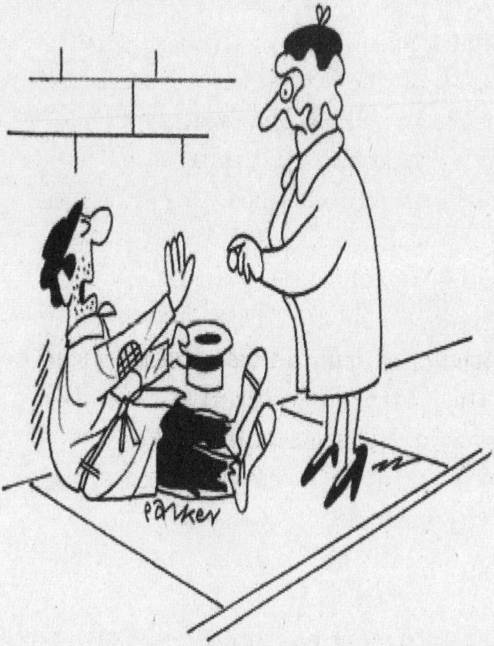

Parker

"Sorry Madam-I'm just closing!"

My Grandpa was killed in Waterloo...Really? Which platform?... Don't be ridiculous! What does it matter which platform!

Tom Stoppard:

What do you call a train full of toffees?

A chew chew.

Rosie age 9

What is the difference between a train and a teacher?

One says "Choo-choo" and the other says,
"Take that gum out of your mouth"

Louis age 12

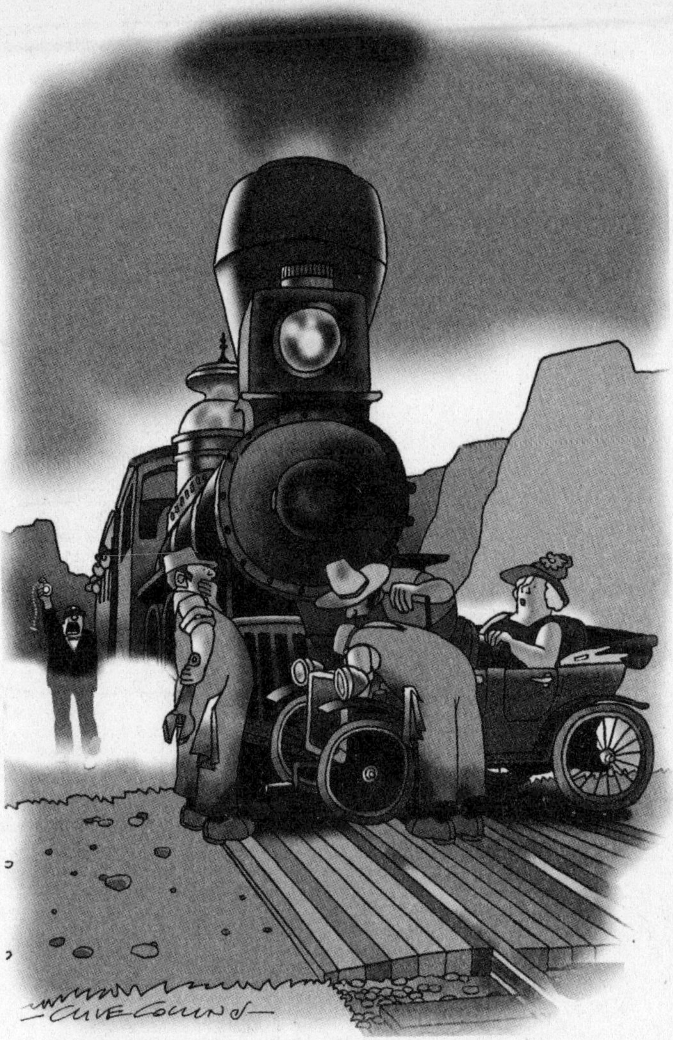

Did you hear about the thief who stole a haggis?
He got off scot free.
Jamie age 14

What do you call two robbers?
A pair of knickers.
Ivo age 8

The man who wrote the hokey cokey was buried yesterday. But they had one problem. They had to put his left leg in and his left leg out!
Luke age 11

There was a man in jail and he wanted to get out, so he dug and dug and he ended up in a playground. He shouted "I'm free" and a little girl said, "ha ha i'm four".
Henry age 6

What do prisoners use to call each other?
Cell phones.
Glenna age 14

192

"My pen leaks!"

How many folk singers does it
take to change a lightbulb?
Five.   One to change the lightbulb and four to sing a
song about how good the old lightbulb was......

How many TV producers does it take
to change a lightbulb?
Does it *have* to be a lightbulb?
Jim Sweeney

What did Geronimo say when he jumped into the lake?
Me!!!
Caleb age 14

There were three people stuck on an island with no food!
They could each have one wish. The first one said 'I
want to go home.' He immediately disappeared. The
second one said the same and he also disappeared. The
third one said 'I'm lonely, I wish they were here!'
Suddenly the other two were back with him on the
island!
Danny age 11

"Hey – nice pad."

Why was the beach wet?
Because the seaweed.
Clementine age 10

What sits on the seabed and shakes?
A nervous wreck.
Grace age 7

What did the shy pebble say?
I wish I was a little boulder.
Lucinda age 10

What gets washed up on really small beaches?
Micro-waves.
Hetty age 9

What did Neptune say when the sea dried up?
I haven't an ocean (notion).
Lydia age 9

HI! YOU'VE REACHED THE SEA - I'M NOT IN RIGHT NOW - PLEASE TRY AGAIN LATER
Davey

What do you call a man floating in sea?
Bob.
Bert age 12

What do you get when you put
a yellow hat into the red sea?
A very wet hat.
Maddie age 14

I think I have
water retention !

What did electrician's wife say to her husband
when he came back home late?
Wire insulate? (Why are you in so late?)
James age 11

What did the string of pearls say to the hat?
You go on ahead, I'll just hang around
Isobel age 9

In which part of town would a
Dressmaker choose to live?
On the outskirts!
Ben age 10

Ladies who Lunch.

Where do you find baby soldiers?
In the infantry.
Harry age 4

How do you get a baby astronaut to sleep?
You rock-et.
Eleanor age 4

What did one tin can say to another?
I've taken a bit of a shine to you.
George age 13

One day two satellites fell in love.
They decided to get married.
The wedding was rubbish but the
reception was amazing!
Tristan age 12

Why don't kangaroo mothers like rainy days?
Because their children have to stay inside.
Jenny age 9

What's black and white, black and white, black and white?
A nun rolling down a hill.
Sasha age 6

What is black and white and red all over?
A newspaper.
Poppy age 14

What did the artist do before she went to bed?
She drew the curtains.
Felicity age 9

What did the Mummy knife say to her baby knife?
Come on, Chip, Chop.
Poppy age 14

Baby balloon wakes up with a bad dream so he goes and gets into bed with his Mum and Dad. He squeezes in between them but there is not enough room. So he lets a bit of air out of his Dad but he is still very squashed, so he lets a bit of air out of his Mum but he is still squashed, so he lets a bit of air out of himself and is finally comfortable and goes fast asleep. Next day when he wakes up his father looks at him and says. "I'm very disappointed with you son not only have you let me down but you've also let your Mum down, but worst of all you've let yourself down."
Stella age 9

Two spitting cobras were out taking a stroll when the son snake turns to the mother snake and asks "Mum! Are we poisonous?"

"Why, yes we are", she replies.

Again the baby snake asks worriedly, "Are you sure we're poisonous?"

"Yes, we are very poisonous".

The baby snake becomes very upset. Again, he asks, "Are we really really poisonous?"

"Yes, we are really really poisonous. In fact we're one of the most poisonous snakes in the world. Why do you ask?"

"I just bit my lip!!!"

Hester age 11

What do polite lambs say to their mothers?
Thank ewe!
Jamie age 2

What did the father shoe say to his cheeky son?
You are having me on!
Thomas age 3

"He's got his father's eyes."

Three sisters ages 102, 104, and 106 live in a house together. One night the 106 year old runs a bath. She puts her foot in and pauses. She shouts down the stairs "was I getting in or out of the bath?"

The 104 year old shouts back "I don't know. I'll come up and see." She starts up the stairs and pauses. Then she yells out "Was I going up the stairs or down?"

The 102 year old is sitting at the kitchen table having tea listening to her sisters. She shakes her head and says "I really hope I never get that forgetful." She knocks on wood for good measure. She then shouts "I'll come up and help both of you as soon as I see who's at the door."

Dylan age 10

"TO THINK ALL THESE YEARS SHE WAS LYING ABOUT HER AGE!"

A man and his wife are woken up at 3 o'clock in the morning, by a loud pounding on the door. The man gets up, puts on his dressing gown and goes down to the door. On the doorstep is a stranger, standing in the pouring rain, rather drunk and asking for a push. The man is furious: "Not a chance," he says "It's 3 o'clock in the morning!" He slams the door shut and returns to bed.

"Who was that?" asked his wife. "Just a drunken guy asking for a push," he answers. "Did you help him?" she asks. "No I did not, it is 3 o'clock in the morning and it is pouring out there!"

"How dare you!" says his wife. "Can't you remember those two guys who came out of their house and helped us? I think you should help him. You should be ashamed of yourself. Go downstairs and help him".

The man does as he is told, gets dressed, opens the front door and goes out into the pouring rain. There is no one there. He calls out into the dark, "Hello, are you still there?" "yesh!" comes back the answer. "Do you still need a push?" calls out the husband. "Yesh please!" comes the reply from the dark. "Well, where are you then? "asks the husband. "I'm over here! On the swing!"

Rupert age 15

the Politician

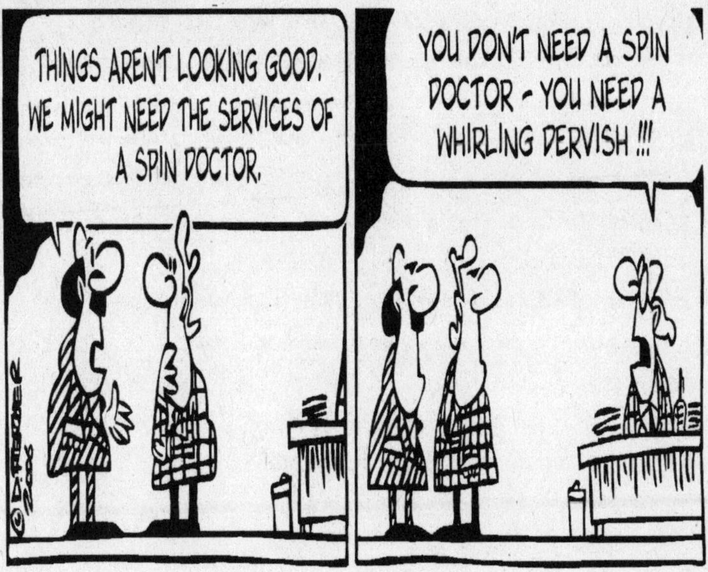
THINGS AREN'T LOOKING GOOD. WE MIGHT NEED THE SERVICES OF A SPIN DOCTOR.
YOU DON'T NEED A SPIN DOCTOR - YOU NEED A WHIRLING DERVISH !!!

What is the difference between a jeweller and a jailor?
One sells watches and the other watches cells.
Isobel age 9

There has been a report that there is a
hole in the wall surrounding the nudist camp.
The Police are looking into the matter.
Johnny age 12

Did you hear about the fool who keeps
going round saying "no"?
No.
Oh, so it's you?
Jasmine age 8

Why is Cinderella bad at football?
Because she ran away from the ball.
Olivia age 16

How do bomb disposal experts dance?
Slow, slow, tick, tick, slow.

Grace age 7

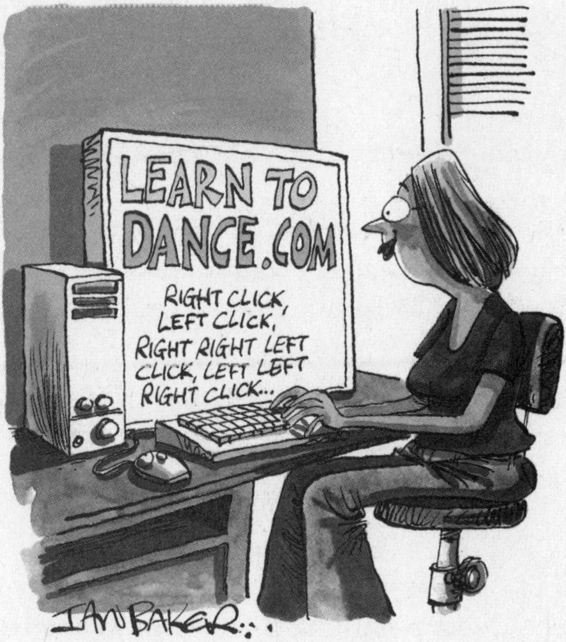
LEARN TO DANCE.COM
RIGHT CLICK, LEFT CLICK, RIGHT RIGHT LEFT CLICK, LEFT LEFT RIGHT CLICK...
IAN BAKER

Why did the coach give his team a lighter?
Because they kept losing their matches.
Roly age 7

Why did the owl fail his exams?
He did not give a hoot.
George age 13

What's the difference between an
iceberg and a clothes brush?
One crushes boats and the other brushes coats.
Joanna age 14

A true story!
"What is an 'idiot'?" enquired the friend. "Oh" replied
my son knowledgably, "that's someone who overtakes
Mummy when she's driving the car!"
Alex age 4

No we're not there yet - Daddy
has to reverse off the drive first

A lady is taking a shower. She hears the doorbell. She looks out of the window and sees that it is the bakery man. She puts on a towel and goes down stairs to collect her loaf of bread. She gets back in the shower. The doorbell goes again - she looks out of the window and sees it is the milkman. She huffs and puffs, puts a towel round her and runs downstairs to collect the milk. She gets back into the shower the doorbell goes again. She looks out of the window, huffs and puffs and sees that it is her neighbour, the blind man. So this time she runs downstairs without her towel opens the door and the blind man says "I have something really exciting to tell you ... I can see again!"

Georgie age 9

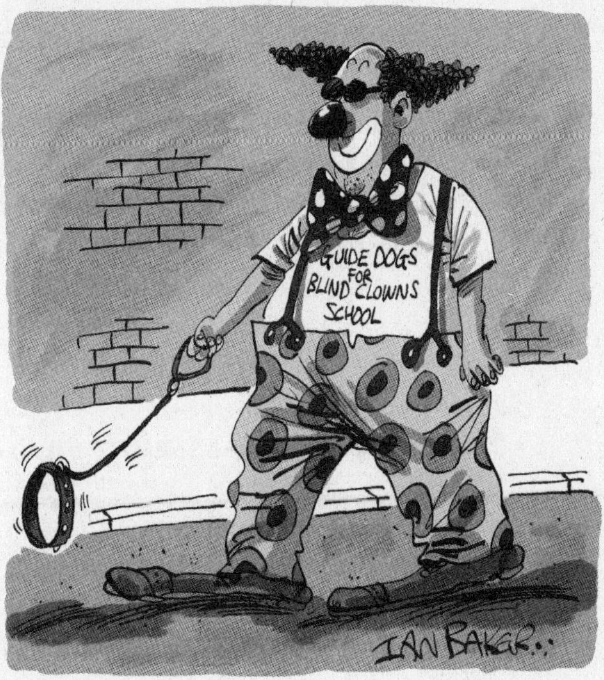
GUIDE DOGS
FOR
BLIND CLOWNS
SCHOOL
IAN BAKER

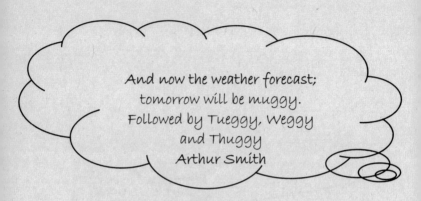

And now the weather forecast;
tomorrow will be muggy.
Followed by Tueggy, Weggy
and Thuggy
Arthur Smith

How do you put an idiot in suspense?
I'll tell you next week!
Fergus age 12

What's brown and sticky?
A stick.
Izzy age 10

What is a chav in a filing cabinet?
Sorted.
Duncan age 12

216

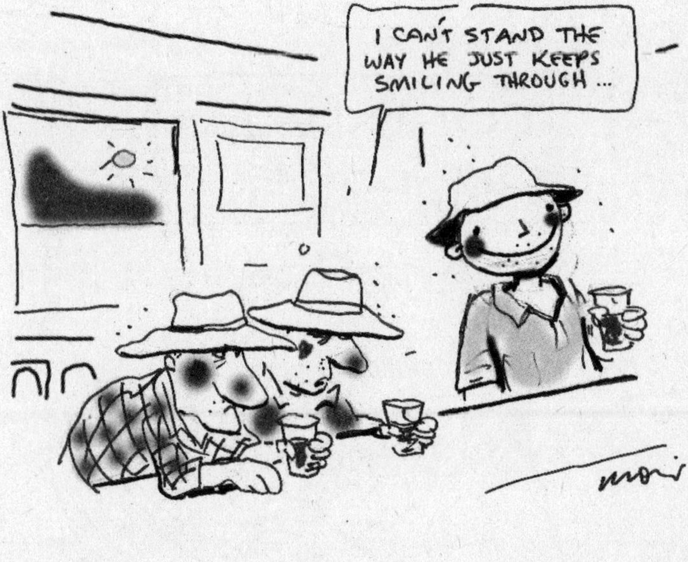
I CAN'T STAND THE WAY HE JUST KEEPS SMILING THROUGH ...

A little boy was attending his first wedding. After the service, his cousin asked him, "How many women can a man marry?"

"Sixteen," the boy responded.

His cousin was amazed that he knew the answer so quickly. "How do you know that?"

"Easy," the little boy said. "All you have to do is add it up, like the vicar said: 4 better, 4 worse, 4 richer, 4 poorer."

Josh age 13

Are you criticizing my driving again ?

How do husbands remember their wife's birthday?
They just have to forget it once.
Camilla age 12

New wife: "will you love me when
I'm old, fat and ugly?"
New husband: "of course I do!"
Dylan age 10

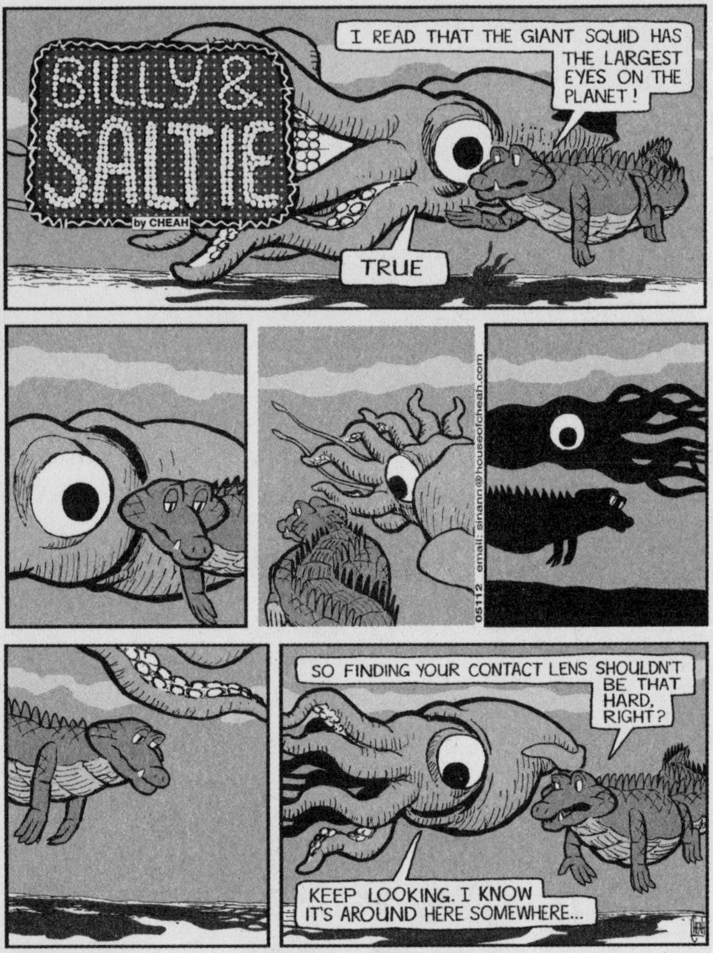
BILLY & SALTIE
by CHEAH
I READ THAT THE GIANT SQUID HAS THE LARGEST EYES ON THE PLANET!
TRUE
05112 email: sinann@houseofcheah.com
SO FINDING YOUR CONTACT LENS SHOULDN'T BE THAT HARD, RIGHT?
KEEP LOOKING. I KNOW IT'S AROUND HERE SOMEWHERE...
CHEAH

A lady was walking in the park when suddenly her left eye flies out. "Oh no" she screams, but luckily a man catches her eye and gives it back to her. She is so pleased that she invites him out to dinner that evening. That night he asks her "why did you invite me out tonight?"

She replies, "You caught my eye."

Flora age 9

How do you get someone up from the ground?
Wind them up!
William age 8

A man goes in to a TV shop and says "Excuse me,
do you have colour TV's for sale?"
The salesman replies "Yes sir, of course
we have colour TV's."
The man replies "Then give me a blue one please."
Shivan age 14

Why did the racing driver make pit stops?
Because it had to ask for directions.
Rosie age 15

What do you do if an idiot throws a grenade at you?
Pick it up, pull out the pin and throw it back.
Fergus age 12

Why shouldn't you race a boxer?
Because they would beat you!
Nicholas age 12

What do you call a man with a spade on his head?
Doug
Thomas age 8

What's a good name for a petrol station attendant?
Phil.
Jamie age 14

What do you call a cowardly knight?
Sir Ender!

A class of boys are going to confession.

The first boy goes into the confessional and says "Bless me Father for I have sinned."
The priest asks him what he has done.
The boy replies "I threw peanuts in the river."
The priest gives him absolution and tells him to say three Hail Mary's as his penance.

The next boy comes into the confessional "Bless me Father for I have sinned... I threw peanuts in the river...."
The boy is given absolution and told to say three Hail Mary's as his penance.

The next boy comes into the confessional "Bless me Father for I have sinned.....I threw peanuts in the river..."
The priest sighs, gives the boy absolution and tells him to say three Hail Mary's.

The next boy comes into the confessional "Bless me Father for I have sinned."
The priest says "let me guess .. you threw peanuts in the river."
The boy says "No, Father, I am Peanuts!"

Sam age 12

What was Noah's profession?
An ark-itect.
Miles age 7

"What's the matter with you boys? You can't even read a blueprint!"

"What do people do to Santa Claus on Christmas Eve?
They give him a round of a pause!
Archie age 10

What is the most popular w(h)ine at Christmas?
"Mummy do I have to eat those Brussels sprouts!"
Lydia age 9

What does Santa use to clean his sleigh?
A ho hose pipe.
Dominic age 6

What do you get if you cross
Father Christmas and a detective?
Santa Clues.
Anthony age 6

226

What do you do if your nose goes on strike?
Picket.
Fergus age 12

"Can you smell snowmen?"

A message from Jenny de Montfort

I would like to thank so many people - in particular Richard Briers, Tim Brooke-Taylor, Sara Cox, Niamh Cusack, Stephen Fry, Tom Stoppard, Arthur Sweeney and Dom Wood for their jokes; Peter Nutsford and Lucy Maxwell have helped at every stage as have Bob and Hazel Cushion at Accent Press; my husband Roger; the amazing children and their parents from all over the world, who took the time to write down their favourite jokes; the cartoonists and illustrators from all over the world and I cannot thank all these contributors enough:

Ian Baker	www.ianbakercartoons.co.uk
Jeremy Banks	www.banxcartoons.co.uk
Steve Breen	San Diego Union-Tribune
Pedro Brock	www.pedroart.co.uk
Rosie Brooks	www.rosiebrooks.co.uk
Simon Chadwick	www.ceratopia.co.uk
Sinann Cheah	www.houseofcheah.com
Clive Collins	www.clivecollinscartoons.com
David Connaughton	www.cartoonists.co.uk/deacon

Jonathan Cusick	www.jonathancusick.com
Andy Davey	www.andydavey.com
Lyn Davies	www.lyndavies.com
Jamie Deuchars	www.cartoonists.co.uk/jamiedeuchars
Robert Duncan	www.duncancartoons.com
Jules Faber	www.julesfaber.com
Chris Field	www.illustrationagency.com/humour
David Fletcher	www.nzcartoons.co.nz
Noel Ford	www.fordcartoon.com
John Graham	www.jgcartoons.co.uk
Bill Houston	www.houstoncartoons.com
James Kemsley	www.gingermeggs.com
Pran Kumar	India
John Landers	www.landers.co.uk
Peter le Vasseur	Guernsey

Mark Lynch	www.cartoons-a-plenty.com
Tony Lopes	The Odd Streak by Tony Lopes
Ron McGeary	www.ronmcgeary.co.uk
Stephen Midgeley	www.jeffref.com
Alan Moir	www.moir.com.au.
Jim Naylor	www.cartoonists.co.uk/naylor
Peter Nesbit	www.cartoonists.co.uk
Richard Newcombe	www.environmentalcartoons.net
Neil Oldham	www.cartoons-humour.fsnet.co.uk
Dave Parker	Bristol, UK
Royston Robertson	www.roystonrobertson.co.uk
William Rudling	www.williamrudling.com
Duncan Scott	www.cartoonists.co.uk/duncanscott
Nik Scott	www.nikscott.com
Kevin Smith	www.CartoonStock.com
Warren Steel	New South Wales, Australia

Nigel Sutherland	www.nigelsutherland.co.uk
Gary Swift	www.garyswift.com
Kate Taylor	www.contact-me.net/KateTaylor
Inglis Thorburn	www.inglisthorburn.com
Stanley Toohey	www.stantoons.co.uk
Geoff Tristram	www.geofftristram.co.uk
Mary West	www.westart.co.uk
Martin Wharmby	London
Tim Whyatt	www.whyatt.com.au
Tom Williams	www.wordgames.co.uk
Mark Wood	www.markwoodcartoonist.co.uk

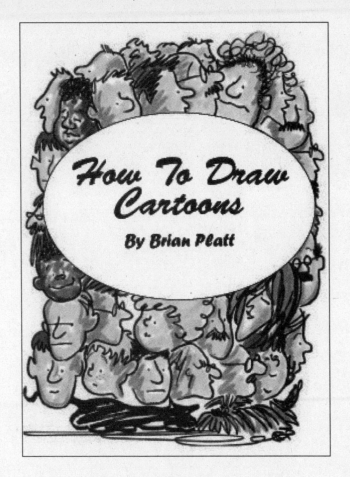

How to Draw Cartoons by Brian Platt
ISBN 9780954709204 price £7.99